Little David

Little David

Elliott Chaze

CHARLES SCRIBNER'S SONS
NEW YORK

Copyright © 1985 Elliott Chaze

Library of Congress Cataloging in Publication Data

Chaze, Elliott.
  Little David.

  I. Title.
PS3505.H633L5   1985   813'.54   85-2074
ISBN 0-684-18286-6

1 3 5 7 9 11 13 15 17 19   H/C   20 18 16 14 12 10 8 6 4 2

Printed in the United States of America.

For Clara Wasson
—a genuine lady

Little David

1

IT WAS RAINING HARD AGAINST THE NARROW WINDOWS AT the far end of the newsroom where Crystal was loading her Nikons and cranking the automatic film advance. Now and again she looked up at Kiel St. James.

She wore the black cashmere turtleneck and gray flannel slacks stuffed into high-heeled boots. The heavy blond hair swung over the gray eyes as she messed with the cameras; and each time she straightened to stare at the city editor she flipped the curtain of hair.

When it rained Crystal somehow looked glossier, almost luminous. And the body language was louder, or so it seemed to St. James. Now he smiled at her as their eyes met. "What you going to shoot, kid? You look like you loaded for bear."

She said nothing, strolling to a filing cabinet and digging around in a drawer. After a time she moved to his desk and sat on the edge of it. She turned the full power of the crushed-glass gaze on him and said, "I can't believe you've started *chewing* tobacco. Your corners are brown. You have the rodeo look."

"There's worse looks."

The newspaper had been put to bed for the final edition and he could feel the humming of the press in the soles of his shoes and the seat of his pants.

"Really, Kiel, *chewing.*" She lifted a foot, holding the long leg stiff. Then she lifted her shoulders, which lifted her breasts, which lifted him inside his corduroys. He could not figure how Crystal could look more exciting in boots than most women who were dressed fit to kill.

"You like my new boots?"

"Sure," he said. "Do we have a date or don't we?"

"Is that all you have to say about them?"

"Yes." He riffled some papers on the desk and said, "Brenda has some like them. She calls them her fuck-me boots."

"She has a foul mouth—I wish you'd smoke a cigarette, Kiel. You look crazy when you don't smoke."

The phone rang and he pretended to be busy with his papers and asked her to answer it. While she talked he filled his eyes with her. And her long body sang its song to him, its long, sliding sweet song.

"It's Orson," she said, pressing the mouthpiece against her breast.

"Tell him I'm busy."

"He wants to talk to *you.*"

"He shit all over us last week on the Bronson story. Tell the sonofabitch to phone the TV people again, maybe they'll take another picture of him squatting beside a burned safe."

"Don't be childish," said Crystal, holding out the phone.

Then he heard the resonant country-preacher voice of the captain of detectives. St. James could see him smirking, spitting into a Dixie cup, feet on desk, wearing that

2

awful lizard-green polyester leisure suit. "Hey, newshound?"

"What you want, Orson?"

"You still mad at me?"

"Why wouldn't I be, you TV-sucking asshole?"

"I'm calling you first on this one, newshound." Boles's voice was aggrieved, theatrically injured; but beneath the banter there was urgency. "We found a body at the city dump."

"Another newborn baby?"

"It's C.B. Barrington."

"The commissioner?"

"None other."

Boles asked the city editor to meet him at the dump on the edge of the sewage-treatment lagoon near the Fox River bridge.

When St. James arrived the county coroner-ranger was squatting beside the body prying something from between the open eyes of the commissioner. Carrington lay on his back in a three-piece suit of gray sharkskin. The razor sharp creases of his pants and the smooth roll of the lapels created the appearance of something happening on the stage of a theater.

Nelson Barton, the coroner-ranger, was scraping at a gummy-looking nugget with the tip of the blade of a murderous-looking jackknife. The steel made a sickening sound against the thing embedded in the bone.

Boles, squatted on the other side of the corpse, winced when the blade made the noise. He nodded at St. James. His lizard-green polyester looked wilted and the smooth ketchup-and-cream complexion darkened as he watched. "My God, Nelson, you been digging in the poor bastard's face a week—can't you get *done* with it?"

3

Nelson said, his voice emotionless, "I think I'm getting it. It's in there deep."

When finally it came out of the bloody socket he blotted it with a bandanna and, laying aside the skinny lock-blade knife, he handed the sticky lump to the captain of detectives. "It looks like a plain damn rock, Orson."

Boles said, "You probably wiped off all the prints you dumb pissant."

Nelson looked hurt.

And Boles, still squatting, holding the plum-sized object on a pad of Kleenex, stared at it as it spread an expanding star of blood into the tissue. "I hate this fucking job," he said to the bloody Kleenex. "I hate every motherfucking thing about it."

St. James hunkered down beside him in the reeking clearing. It was still raining lightly and the droplets thinned the blood in the socket between the commissioner's staring eyes and turned pink in the overflow. Barrington's ear was filled with the pink juice and he seemed to be glaring at the Kleenex.

"Orson, it is a rock, isn't it?"

"Well as I can tell."

"How in God's name could anyone sink a rock that size in the bone?"

"I don't know."

"A rubber-powered slingshot wouldn't do it, you think?"

Orson Boles stood up. "Dunno." Then he turned to the Rescue Eight team which had placed Barrington on a stretcher for the trip to the ambulance. "Put something over his face, for Christsake."

When the others were gone St. James and Boles sat side by side on a wooden crate stamped HONDA. It commenced raining harder and a rat popped out of a peach

4

can and sat down and watched them, its naked tail looking raw and clean. "Poor little bastard," said Boles of Barrington. "Everything he touched turned to shit."

Boles got up and prowled around, studying the cluttered, muddy ground in the clearing. He scribbled some notes on a pad, the rain bouncing off the pad and splattering against his brutal crew cut, darkening the green polyester leisure suit.

Finally they went to Boles's car and sat for a time talking. They discussed at some length the kind of weapon required to propel a rock with enough velocity to do what the rock had done. "I never saw a nigger-shooter that would do it," said the detective. The rock lay on the dashboard of the Chevy, still resting on the Kleenex, the star-shaped stain almost black now.

St. James winced at the words nigger-shooter and Boles said, "I meant to say *Negro*-shooter. I keep forgetting you're one a them knee-jerk liberals."

2

CRYSTAL ARRIVED IN HER BATTERED OLD JAGUAR SHORTLY before dusk and they sat in the sling chairs on his front porch sipping beer and watching the squirrels pop their tails.

Crystal said she had dropped by Mixon's Funeral Home and that Barrington's widow, Nina, was squirting tears all over the place. "She seems truly sad," said Crystal. "And everybody knows that she and C.B. hated each other's guts. When I was there they were still working on the body. They have to fill that hole between his eyes with wax and it has to be just the right color to blend with his skin."

St. James made a face, thinking of the rain splatting the cavity between Barrington's eyes.

"Let's talk about something else," St. James said. He tried to leer at her but couldn't bring it off. He felt about as lustful as a salted snail.

"Okay," said Crystal. "We shall talk about the squirrels. Or shall be talk about going inside and going to bed?"

"Make it squirrels."

"They are so electric," said Crystal. "Can you imagine being able to run headfirst down a tree?"

"No."

"Are they promiscuous? You never see them in the act of copulation. Do they feel a sense of responsibility to their mates? And to their offspring? Or is the family simply accidental and perhaps convenient?"

"Probably."

"Does a male think that the female of his choice is cuter than other females? Does he get a lump in his throat when he watches her flow along a power line or silently pop her tail high in an oak? In his eyes is she truly distinctive and preferable to other females?"

A squirrel scampered up an early blooming Japanese magnolia onto the vacant house next door, running along the tiled ridge-line, a fluttering blur of cream and taupe. Then motionless against a darkening opaline sky of rose and lavender, the tail high against the back and looped like the handle of a teacup. St. James kept a pair of binoculars beside his chair for squirrel and birdwatching. Through the binoculars he could see the individual hairs on the squirrel, the gleaming bulge of the eyes. It leaped lightly into an oak, then onto a power cable, loping along the cable and jumping onto a limber twig, jouncing, obviously enjoying it.

"What do they think about?" said Crystal. "Sex? Food? They can't be hungry. There are so many acorns in the yard that it's like walking on ball bearings. Probably sex?"

"Probably."

"Do you ever think about sex, Kiel? Or do you simply sit in your chair and guzzle tepid beer?"

Happily, he had commenced thinking about sex. Thinking very hard about it, in fact.

They went into the house and went to bed.

7

3

BRENDA KEETON, THE POLICE REPORTER, WAS SEVERELY pissed about the fact St. James had not called her in on the story at the very beginning.

"You throw a wad of notes at me and I can't even read your handwriting." Her lips looked bitten and she was pregnant again. Whenever her lips looked bitten for a couple of weeks or so she got pregnant and was sick in the mornings, spending a great deal of time in the ladies' restroom. Her clear green eyes had brown bruises beneath them, apparently a genetic thing which had not been visible until she put away her spectacles for contact lenses.

"Orson told me to come out to the dump alone," said St. James, knowing that he should have alerted Brenda. He picked up the phone and dialed Orson Boles and said to the captain of detectives, "Give Brenda everything you have on the Barrington thing, start from the beginning, will you Orson?"

"Are you crazy?" said Boles. "You think all I got to do is talk to reporters?"

"As a personal favor, Orson."

"You was there, hoss, I told you every fucking thing I know—which is nothing."

When the detective hung up the phone St. James turned to the stocky police reporter, whom he dearly loved and respected, and said, "Write the goddamned story, Brenda."

"He wouldn't talk to me?"

"Write the story. I'll help you with the notes."

"The lousy bristle-headed motherfucker," said Brenda.

She wrote her page-one streamer story and punched it into the computer sytem, which promptly swallowed it, and refused to yield it for editing. As always, it was maddening and happened on the very edge of deadline for the first edition. St. James despised the new noiseless journalism which substituted video display terminals for typewriters. In the old days when they lost something in the composing room you could go back there and vent your spleen on the composing-room foreman, a crusty, cadaverous veteran of the hot-type era, who as often as not would tell you to kiss his ass. And now the electronic memory bank, a gray metal box, just sat there silently. You could not even beat on it because it was quite delicate and expensive.

About fifteen minutes before the 10:30 A.M. deadline the memory bank decided to relinquish Brenda's piece on the Barrington killing and it was a thorough story, insofar as the facts permitted, complete with the obituary material attached to the tail end. Barrington had been married five times, siring a single child by each wife. None, with the exception of Nina and her daughter, Willa Mae, lived in Catherine and none of the out-of-town survivors attended the funeral the following day.

The Reverend Johnny Quick officiated at the funeral at the Trinity Methodist Church. Quick, who at one time in his climb to better things had been an enlisted man in

9

the navy and had a tattoo on his right forearm, leaned to nautical language whenever it could be used. He said that C.B. Barrington was "shipping out on a new and exciting voyage," far beyond the "heavy seas and foul weather of this experience of the flesh."

The pallbearers were the mayor, the inside commissioner, and six policemen, Boles among them. He winked at St. James as the coffin was carried out of the sanctuary for the trip to the cemetery. Brenda, who was standing beside St. James, glared at Boles and hissed, "You lousy jerk."

4

BOLES WAS CLEANING THE SLIDE OF A GOVERNMENT ISSUE Colt .45 automatic. He had stripped the handgun down to its basic parts, disassembling everything but the trigger assembly. The barrel, lying on an oily towel with the other stuff, looked strangely naked without the blunt-nosed slide. The banana smell of Hoope's cleaning oil was strong in the room.

"I tell you, hoss," said Boles, his blue eyes on the work at hand, "I don't have the first solid clue on C.B.'s murder."

"It's been two weeks," said St. James. "You ought to have *something*."

"We sent the rock off to the state crime lab, like I told you. It had traces of gunpowder on it, would you believe that?"

"I believe it, but why in the hell didn't you tell me in time for today's paper?"

Boles grinned brilliantly, laying the oily slide on the towel. "Now don't get your ugly feathers up, hoss. We just got the report."

11

"And we'll hear all about it on the six o'clock news. Orson, if you do that to me again you're on my permanent shit-list."

Boles was sweating lightly in the warm room. He was wearing a lavender short-sleeved button-down shirt with green pants and a mustard-colored necktie of incredible width. His reddish brown hair was cut so short you could see the gleam of his moist scalp and he was chewing an unlit cigar the size of a relay-runner's baton. "You know anything about Centipede grass, hoss?"

"I don't give a hoot about Centipede grass," said the editor. "Is your report going to be on the six o'clock news?"

Boles picked up the olive-steel slide from the towel and peered into it, grinning, obviously enjoying the situation. "Fellow tells me that Centipede will grow damn near anywhere. I've tried everything else, Bermuda, St. Augustine, even Bahia and oats. Not even the national debt would grow in my yard."

"Fuck your yard."

Boles widened his eyes in mock shock. "Sometimes you ain't a nice person, Kiel—sometimes you are not a nice person at all." He put on his country-preacher, cornpone accent and richened the resonance. His ketchup-and-cream complexion glowed with pleasure.

"You give this stuff to television this afternoon and you will have to die to get your name in *The Catherine Call*, Orson."

Boles stuffed a rag into the hollow U-shaped slide and jiggled it. "Keep your pants on," he said. "Try to give me some help, hoss. I can get my ass chewed out at home. You figure the rock was fired from a gun? Maybe a shotgun?"

"I don't know."

"You used to help me, hoss. Now all you do is sit around and pout about the TV."

Despite himself, St. James was drawn into the details of the puzzle. "Why wouldn't the killer simply shoot Barrington with an ordinary shell, a load of buckshot. Blow his head off?"

"That's what I keep asking myself."

"Let me see the rock, Orson."

Boles opened a drawer and fished out the smooth brown and white stone. "It's too big for a 12-gauge. It might a come out the end of an old-timey buffalo gun, say a Sharps, but I doubt it."

"I think you're right," said Kiel St. James, rolling the stained stone about on the desk blotter, using the tip of a ballpoint pen. "You've got to be right. You could split the plastic shell and force this in after the regular load was removed—but it wouldn't fit in the receiver."

Brenda Keeton did not knock on the closed door. She stalked up to Boles's desk, ignoring St. James, staring down with distaste at the oily mess of gun parts on the desk. Her lips looked puffed and bitten and she was only a little pregnant. Later she would be very pregnant. *The Catherine Call*'s intrepid police reporter could get madder and pregnanter than anybody in St. James's memory. She was pale with anger, the brown bruises beneath her eyes floating like dead leaves on a pond of cream.

Boles looked up from his disassembled .45 and grinned, "Why hallo there, Sugar Britches."

"I see we're having another goddamned summit meeting," Brenda hissed. "Why aren't you taking notes, Kiel?"

"What's eating you, kid?" said St. James.

"She's always mad," Boles grinned. "She was born mad, weren't you, honey?"

13

Brenda rested her weight on the flats of her hands on the desk. "You keep going over my head to Kiel and you'll see what mad really is, you devious, TV-loving wimp."

"Now, now," purred Boles. "Now, now, honey."

"Don't honey me. I don't want any favors or any of your sweet talk. I just want a square deal." She turned her head to glare at St. James. "I'm the only police reporter in Alabama who has to compete with her boss on a goddamn murder case."

St. James felt his hackles begin to rise; but he recognized at the same time that her anger was legitimate. He asked her to sit down and when she did he described in detail what he and Boles had been talking about. "It's a mystery to both of us," he concluded. "The rock doesn't make sense. Does it to you?"

Obviously mollified, Brenda said no. She lit a cigarette and leaned back in her chair. "So where does this leave us?"

"It doesn't leave us anywhere," said Boles, dropping the banter and the grin. He could turn it on and off. "We can't even figure what kind of weapon could handle that kind of ballistics. Even if he managed to cram it into the receiver of a 10-gauge shotgun it would probably blow the barrel to smithereens. You can lose face that way. I mean your *whole* face."

"The killer has to be some kind of a nut," said St. James to Brenda, not apologizing to her in words, the apology in his tone of voice. "In any case we're stumped."

"Stalled," said Boles. "Not stumped."

"Okay, we're stalled."

"I talked with a Miz Edgarton," said Boles. "She lives about a quarter-mile from the dump and she saw the commissioner headed out that way in his blue Plymouth a couple of hours before the kids found the body. The

14

boys were looking for aluminum cans. They wore Nike jogging shoes and their footprints were all over the place until the rain washed them out. We found only two other sets of footprints in the clearing where C.B. was killed. One set belonged to him and one set was barefeet, about a size eight. The commissioner's prints came straight from the Plymouth to the clearing, maybe fifty yards. The barefoot prints came from the edge of the lagoon and we lost 'em there in the mud."

Boles said the barefoot prints were made by feet with very high arches. He grinned and said, "All we have to do is locate everybody in the area with high insteps who were barefoot at the time and happened to be at the city dump."

"And you're still certain the homicide occurred where the body was found?" said St. James.

"Yep."

"And you think the stone was fired from the barrel of some kind of gun," said Brenda.

"Yep."

"It doesn't make sense," said Brenda.

"Not a frazzlin' bit," said Boles.

5

MAYOR LEON LINK HAD OUTLIVED HIS BRAIN. HE LOOKED fifteen years younger than his seventy years; but the lights had gone out upstairs and he awoke in a new world every day.

His dentures were an excellent fit and it was said that he could eat apples and corn on the cob. He smiled constantly. St. James found it mildly disconcerting when he asked the mayor if he knew anyone who hated C.B. Barrington enough to kill him.

Link grinned whitely and said, "There was a lot of folks that got put out with C.B. Mostly they was mad about the topsoil."

"Topsoil?"

"Yass, you would be surprised how mad people can get over topsoil. They would phone C.B. in the middle a the night and say why didn't he bring the load of topsoil he promised. Would you like a cigar, Mister, ah . . ."

"St James," said St. James, "Kiel St. James."

"Oh, yass, you Leonard St. James's boy."

"No, sir, that's another St. James."

"Leonard was blind, he use to tune our piano. Couldn't see a damn thing and he make that piano sing. How're things over at WDOX?"

"I'm not with the TV station, I'm with the newspaper."

"Hell, I knew that. How 'bout a cigar?"

"No thank you, sir. Do you remember any of the people who were upset over not getting any topsoil?"

"Just about everybody that's got a yard, son. It wasn't only that they couldn't *get* topsoil, it was after they got it they would find old bicycle seats and condoms and roots and brambles ten feet long. C.B. give me some topsoil for my side yard and I found a half a pair of pliers, broken bottles and brickbats, half a dead mouse, even one a them things that the girls twirl in the marching band. You name it and I found it. Plumb wear you out just cleaning the garbage out the dirt."

Despite himself, St. James was drawn into the idiotic flow of an interview which appeared headed nowhere. "You wouldn't think people would get all that angry over a pile of dirt," he said lamely, talking through a swirling screen of the mayor's cigar smoke. "Did anyone threaten C.B.? I mean, to your knowledge?"

"Not's I know. How's ya dad, he still tuning them pianos?"

"You and C.B. were old fishing buddies," said St. James. "He trusted you with certain confidences he'd share with few others, isn't that correct?"

"Say what?"

"Did he indicate at any time during your joint tenure on the city council that someone—one of his enemies, political or otherwise—might want to kill him?"

"I don't know anybody would want to *kill* C.B. Maybe slap him around a mite, or kick him in the nuts."

17

"Okay, who wanted to slap him around?"

The mayor stubbed out his cigar and looked at his watch, a massive gold Rolex that looked as big as a manhole cover on the bony wrist. He squinted against smoke and grinned and said, "Coffee time, Bub, you want some coffee?"

"Thank you, no."

"I can still hear ya dad plinking that piano. Blind as a bat. A artist. That's what Leonard was, a artist if ever there was one."

"My father's dead," said St. James. "He wasn't blind. You didn't know him. And he never tuned your fucking piano."

The mayor's secretary entered with coffee and doughnuts on a tray as St. James departed. She set the tray on Link's desk and he said, "What got *his* tail up in the air, for Petesake?"

"I don't know," she said. "He seemed to be in a fine humor when he came in."

St. James drove directly to the Barrington residence after leaving City Hall. Nina answered his knock. She was wearing a pink nylon housecoat with little brown sea horses printed on it. She led him into the living room and sat on a couch, patting the place beside her, crossing her legs and trying to look flustered when the housecoat slid open to mid-thigh.

"It was nice of you to come by, Kiel," she said. "But I've told about everything I know to Captain Boles."

St. James, "Yes ma'am, I hate to bother you, but maybe you can tell me some things we need to know. Had anybody threatened the commissioner that you know?"

"Not as I know." She pursed pale fat lips and frowned

down at her bare thigh but did not make an effort to cover it.

"Take your time and really think about it."

She frowned at her thigh for a while and finally pulled the nylon over it. "There was some trouble about gravel."

"Gravel?"

"C.B. use to sneak some gravel into the driveways of people he really liked—or people he could use."

"I didn't know that."

"He wasn't supposed to," she said. "But he did it. And this man kept phoning and saying he knew damn well some people got it and why couldn't he expect equal treatment. He got real nasty."

"Did he threaten your husband?"

"I don't know about that."

"Do you know the man's name?"

"No, C.B. simply mentioned that the fellow acted pretty ugly. He didn't say a lot to me about his business —or anything else. He wasn't here much except for supper and to sleep. Most days he just drove around watching his crews work on the streets, or he was at some funeral home so he could sign his name on the guest-book. You know, so the family of the deceased would see his name and vote for him when the time came. He never really cared, if you ask me. He didn't even attend the funerals, just popped in and out and said how sorry he was and patted the widow."

"That wins votes?"

"C.B. said it did. He said it was even better than kissing a baby on the head."

"Maybe he was right."

"There must have been something to it," said Nina, moving her leg so that the nylon slid open again. "He was reelected four times you know."

19

"Yes, ma'am, he was for sure."

"He didn't let on much about his worries. He believed in putting on a happy face."

This was an understatement. C.B. Barrington laughed when he told you hello. St. James had known him for years and marveled at the fact a man in his late sixties could be so steadily cheerful in a job packed with headaches and worse. But it was the truth. Barrington always looked as happy as a dog with two dicks. When he and the mayor were seated at the same table during the regular weekly meeting of the city council, both of them grinning and laughing, laughing at the bids on gasoline for city vehicles, laughing at the new budget, laughing at announcements of retirements and pension benefits, it was unreal.

Barrington looked a great deal like the late Claude Rains and most women found him attractive. He rode a black horse in college homecoming parades and was proud of the fact he was country-bred. He was a frugal man and the horse, which a friend kept for him south of town, was one of his few extravagances. He bragged on the mileage he could get out of a dollar. If you bought a car, he knew where you could have gotten it cheaper. Or a suit, or a steak, anything. Once he and Nina went to New York to see a sick relative and C.B. said they found a bus that would take them from their hotel to the airport for four dollars, when taxi-fare was thirty-four dollars. He saw a Broadway play for half price by standing in a special line in Times Square. He found a restaurant which served a hearty breakfast for $1.95 and another that sold po-boy beef sandwiches for less than they cost in Catherine. He located a $45-a-day hotel. "First class place," he laughed as if it were the funniest thing in the world. Then, pursing his lips, "I reckon I'm what you'd have to call a country-slicker, heh?" When he had his prostate removed, he went to the Veterans Administration Hospital fifty miles south of Catherine. He procured free dentures and spectacles from the VA. In good weather he rode a bicycle to work, a distance of several miles. "Get fifty miles on a Pepsi," he laughed. He didn't truly talk. He laughed his words out. Admirers, and they were remarkably numerous, claimed that a few years back C.B. was a master cocksman and that even at sixty-eight he got his share. Mostly from widows he comforted at Mixon's Funeral Home.

St. James hesitated to ask the question, but did it anyway. "Were there any jealous husbands?"

"Probably," said Nina Barrington to her white naked leg. "He had a way with women, you know that. He didn't do his homework, but he pleased a bunch of women that didn't really know him. I never worried about what he was doing with his *thing*. If you can't get it up, it can't get out, now can it?"

"I guess not," said St. James, avoiding Nina's eyes. They were large and lusterless, the curious color of pralines.

"Could you name anybody?"

She thought about that for a time and said finally, "Maybe Dillard Harmon."

"Who's that?"

"He's chief mechanic at the City Barn. He keeps the patrol cars and the garbage trucks and all that running. He's maybe fifty and married to a twenty-three–year-old redhead. She's in heat. I mean seven days a week. Anybody. Everybody."

"Is Harmon a violent man?"

"I don't know about that. All I know about him really is in connection with his work."

21

"And what's that?"

"C.B. said he's the best mechanic in the state of Alabama, bar none. If it's broke, he can fix it. That's what C.B. said."

"Did the commissioner have anything to do with Mrs. Harmon, I mean, to your knowledge?"

"I think he messed around with her in the sand traps at the Country Club a few times, but I'm not sure. She and C.B. rubbed all over each other on the dance floor and I saw Dillard watching them. He didn't look too happy about it. And C.B. would take her outside at intermission. One night when we got home I was looking for money and found sand in his pockets."

"Oh?"

"Sometimes I had to beg him for money to run the house. He was mean with money. When he had to buy Willa Mae's graduation dress you'd've thought he was financing the Panama Canal diggings."

"You're his fifth wife?"

"As far as I know. I got the cannon when most a the ammunition was gone. I guess my mother was right about him."

"What do you mean?"

"She said never trust a man with little hands and feet and a straight part in his hair."

"About Dillard Harmon, I didn't know the Country Club leaned to mechanics, to working men," said Kiel St. James.

"They don't, but Dillard's the only man in the county that can fix their Volvos and Porsches. He don't even pay dues. His drinks are free. You see a Mercedes Benz in this town it's got Dillard's wrench-marks on it."

"If it's broke he can fix it."

"You better believe it. He's got my seventy-three Caddy runnin' like a Swiss clock. He can fix anything except that little redheaded slut, Stephanie. Dillard doesn't play golf, but they say Stephanie's been in every sand trap on that eighteen-hole course."

"Maybe she's the nineteenth hole."

"You could say that," said Nina Barrington. "I believe half the men have played it." She smiled and crinkled the praline-colored eyes. "It's so easy to make."

6

DILLARD HARMON WAS A SALLOW SIX-FOOTER. HIS LONG face wore the resigned, irritable mask peculiar to automotive mechanics.

St. James felt curiously humble in the presence of men who knew how to fix automobiles. He himself was hard put to change a flat tire, and he felt the weight of his ignorance now as he introduced himself to Harmon and shook hands.

"What can I do for you?" Harmon said. He sucked the bleeding knuckle of a thumb, his eyes round and cool.

"I know you're busy, Mr. Harmon, but I'd like to talk to you about C.B. Barrington."

Harmon said nothing. He blotted his thumb against the bib of his overalls. His face reflected neither distaste nor anticipation. The thumb continued to bleed.

"Is that okay with you?" said St. James.

Someone cranked the engine of a dump truck down the line.

"I don't mind," said Harmon, "but make it snappy."

24

He waved at the line of open-jawed trucks and police cars. "I'm up to my ass in bumblebees."

"For starters," said St. James, "how well did you know the commissioner?"

"I fixed his wife's car a couple a times."

"Were you social friends, I mean off the job?"

"Wait a minute," said Harmon. His cheekbones reddened. "What's this all about you coming in here acting like Dickless Tracy?"

"I'm trying to help Captain Boles," said St. James. "Did you see the commissioner the day he was killed? That morning? Before the homicide?"

"Naw."

"When did you last see him?"

"Hell, I don't know; he was in and out of here a dozen times a week. Most weeks. I guess I saw him out at the club the Saturday night before the Monday that they found his body."

"Then you *were* social friends?"

"If you call dancing on the same floor being social friends."

"Did you have any reason to dislike him?"

Harmon fished a heavy, open-end wrench from a hip pocket and wiped it against a grease-gray palm. "What you saying?"

"I'm not saying anything."

Harmon sighed. "You wasting your time mister and mine, too."

St. James smiled: "I've got time to *burn.*"

"Well don't burn it *here.*"

"Why're you so upset?"

"I'm not upset." Harmon drew a slow, long breath and closed his eyes. "I didn't like that sonofabitch when he was alive—and I don't like him any more now that he's dead."

"Why didn't you like him?"

"Take off, bud." It was plain that he meant it. St. James thanked him for his time and turned to leave, trying not to look as if he was being run off. He felt a sense of extreme embarrassment, not because of the mechanic's hostility, but because the interrogation had been handled so clumsily. He felt that any cub reporter or rookie cop could have brought it off more intelligently, with less obvious intent. Thank God Brenda hadn't heard him. He simply wasn't at his best in the presence of mechanics. It was ever thus. A long history of frustration and defeat at the hands of men who understood or at least pretended to understand the mysteries of carburetors, drive shafts, and alternators. He felt the same way in the presence of plumbers and carpenters, but not quite so intensely. He forced himself to walk slowly the length of the huge Quonset hut and out into the sunshine of late March. In the back of his head he could hear Boles laughing—laughing his ass off.

Driving back to the office he thought of all the questions he should have asked and didn't and of the ones he shouldn't've asked and did. The town was beautiful this time of year. Bursting with color and the rising juices of regeneration, bright with wisteria and jonquil and azalea, heartbreakingly lovely with the oaks greening and everything smelling fresh and new. Then his thoughts turned to Crystal, to the long sweet curves of her where it was always spring.

It was late afternoon when he parked his car in the lot behind the county courthouse and walked across the street to the regional jail complex. The gray Honda hatchback was new and he paused for a time to admire it. It was a fine piece of machinery and he loved it.

Boles's desk, always cluttered, looked worse than usual.

Identifiable objects included a black rubber inner tube, a muddy leather boot, long rawhide thongs, and a forked branch from a tree. There also was a red net bag filled with marbles and a ball of twine.

"You just in time, hoss," Boles beamed. He was cutting strips from the inner tube with a pair of kindergarten scissors. It appeared to be tough going, the protruding tip of Boles's tongue moving more or less in the direction he wished to make the cut.

"Just in time for what?"

"You'll see."

"Golly-gee, I can't *wait*."

"Don't be ugly, hoss." Boles slammed the blunt-nosed kiddy scissors down on the desk. The bag of marbles jumped and chattered against the formica. "Reba, god-dammit, find me a pair a *scissors*," the detective bellowed, his secretary appearing almost immediately in the open doorway.

"Is something wrong?" said Reba Waldoff in her quietest voice. The louder Boles got the quieter Reba got and it never failed to infuriate him.

"I got to cut this rubber," said Boles. "I am not making paper chains or little paper ducks."

"I didn't know," Reba whispered, smiling sweetly. "You just never know around here."

She disappeared and returned soon with a pair of heavy-duty scissors. She laid them on the desk and said, "You know, I can't read your *mind*, Orson."

"There isn't just a whole bunch there to read," said St. James. Then, as Reba left the room, he said, "Orson, any jackass would know you're making a slingshot, right?"

"Apparently," said Boles.

"Why the rawhide bootlaces?"

"I'm going to make both kinds, hoss, a rubber-powered

27

job and a real old-timey sling that you whirl round your head. You know, David and Goliath.''

"And what do you get out of all that?''

"I want to test velocities.''

"Neanderthal ballistics, that's far out.''

Boles became completely serious. "The back inner tubes they make nowadays have about as much flex as asphalt. No zing. When I was a kid they had pink inner tubes of live rubber that would whizz a rock out of sight.''

"Why aren't you talking cornpone today?'' said St. James. "I love it when you forget your country-preacher, Good-Ole-Boy act.''

"Never mind that,'' said Boles. "I just wish I could find me one a them *pink* inner tubes.''

He said that he would cut the rock-pocket from the tongue of the boot and trim the forked branch down to size and power it with the strips of rubber. He would cut another rock-pocket for the traditional sling, which of course would be powered by the thongs alone. "My dad made me one a long time ago and I got pretty good with it. You have a loop that goes around your middle finger and at the end of the other thong you make a big knot that you pinch between the thumb and index finger. You whirl it overhead a few times with the weight of the rock in the pocket and centrifugal force holding it there and then you turn loose a the knot and *whoosh*.''

"Sounds pretty tricky.''

"It is, the trick is to turn loose a the knot at exactly the right time so the rock heads for the target.''

St. James felt his interest quickening. But he said, "It sounds like an awfully unreliable murder weapon.''

"Not in the right hands, hoss.''

"And you have the right hands?''

"I used to, back on the farm. I could scare hell out of a flying crow when I was fifteen.''

"The commissioner wasn't *scared* to death, Orson."

"I know that, hoss—but he wasn't flying either, now *was* he?"

"What about the gunpowder? You said it looked as if the stone was fired from a weapon."

"The state crime lab said that. I'm setting aside the gunpowder for now."

"How can you do that?"

"The lab people said they found no striations on the rock, no marks to support the theory the missile came from a gun. Nothing. Only the gunpowder and some smears of algae."

"Aren't you going at it from the wrong end, Orson? Shouldn't you be talking to people who knew C.B.? Or looking for the source of the stone?"

"There are ten thousand places an hour's drive from Catherine where you can find the same smooth white stones. Every gravel pit swarms with 'em. Igneous rocks, basically quartz. Worn smooth by water. By the by, I hear you been talking to Miz Barrington and Dillard Harmon, hoss."

"You asked me to try to help."

"That's right, newshound, you been helpful more than once in the past. I just want you to know I keep an eye on you."

"Are you tailing me?"

"Now and again, I don't want you hurt."

"Who's going to hurt me, the mechanic?"

"I don't know. I just know you won't be much help to me if you turn up with a rock between your pretty blue, bloodshot eyes."

"Stoned?"

"That too," said Orson Boles, the tip of his tongue following the cut of the rubber.

29

7

WHILE HE WAS BATHING AND SHAVING FOR HIS DATE WITH Crystal the phone rang three times and three times he ignored it. The fourth time he loped into the bedroom and answered it. For a time there was no response. As he was about to chock the phone into its cradle he heard low laughter at the other end of the line and a muffled male voice said: "That you?"

"You *who?*" The lights were off except in the bathroom and St. James suddenly felt more naked, chilly. The skin tightened over his ribs and he shivered, the damp towel around his waist loosening and falling on his bare feet. "Who *is* this?" he said.

"It's me, sport, it's Little David."

"David who?" Realizing the asininity of the dialogue and suspecting a practical joke, St. James relaxed and began laughing. His naked knees looked enormous in the reflected light from the bathroom. He wanted a cigarette, the craving suddenly all over him like rain, his lungs crying for a Kool Filter King.

The voice said flatly, unrecognizably, "You on the wrong side, bud."

Still halfway suspecting a joke, St. James said, "The wrong side of what?"

"You know what I mean, we been watching you."

"Join the club, *every*body's watching me. Who the hell *is* this, anyway?" It sounded a little like Briscoe Risk, the special assignments reporter. Only a little. The voice had no clean edges. Apparently it was filtered through a handkerchief or something.

No answer.

"Identify yourself or hang up," said St. James. "I got no time for any more of this kind of foolishness. Is that you, Briscoe?"

"And David put his hand in his bag, and took thence a stone," intoned the voice, deepening on the final word of the sentence. "And he *slang* it and smote the Philistine in his forehead, that the stone sunk into his forehead; and he fell upon his face to the earth."

"Orson, Orson is that you?" said St. James. "It's got to be you, you crazy clown."

The phone clicked off at the other end of the line.

"Orson?"

But the phone was dead.

He dialled Boles's home number and waited, the water of his bath evaporating so that he could see the steam coming off his chest in the cool room. He tucked in his chin and stared slantingly at his knees. Were they *growing*? Did one's knees continue to grow throughout a lifetime? Like noses and ears and fingernails? Did quitting cigarettes enlarge your knees? Boles, you bastard, where are you? The phone rang a half-dozen times before he gave up.

He got dressed and drank a dose of I. W. Harper,

standing at the kitchen sink and chasing it with tapwater. Then he chased the tapwater with a stingingly cold bottle of Miller's beer and when that was accomplished he ransacked the house looking for a cigarette. In the end he stuffed a wad of Red Man in his cheek, blotting the corners of his mouth when he heard Crystal at the door. The chewing tobacco gave him a degree of relief; but Crystal would not kiss him and he had to establish his priorities before answering the doorbell. The chew of Red Man or a kiss from Crystal. The hell with kissing, he could get around to that later.

The first thing she said when he let her in was about what he expected, "Your corners are brown."

"The rodeo look?" He smiled squishily.

"Worse than that."

They went to the kitchen and he opened a beer for Crystal and they sat at the table, he unable to drink until he was finished with the juicy cud. He had to be very careful to swallow in the back of his throat, not to involve any of the mess up front. It could make you very sick if you forgot and swallowed from the front. "Wusha noo good?" he said.

Crystal did not want to make love.

Crystal did not want to talk about the Barrington murder.

She did appear faintly interested in the weird phone call and said that it had to be Boles, that it was the kind of thing he would do—which, of course, it was.

Crystal wanted to drink quite a lot of beer, which they managed to do with a minimum of conversation. She looked painfully young tonight in her faded khaki shorts and turquoise sweatshirt, a loose fitting thing which allowed a great deal of bobbling of pointed breasts and emphasized the slender roundness of her. She wore no socks, old white sneakers, and a pair of absurdly large plastic-jade earrings which hung down in loops almost to her collarbones as she hunched over her cold beer at the rickety kitchen table.

Why did he find peace and reassurance with this strange child? At his age? What really did they have in common beside the very good sex and an unseemly appetite for alcohol and home made chili? He had a pot of his special chili bubbling on the stove; but Crystal said she wasn't hungry and this suited him because he had forgotten to buy fresh soda crackers. Chili was nothing without crisp crackers.

What Crystal wanted to do was walk.

So they walked.

Timothy Lane was fairly well illuminated by the streetlights and as they passed houses where people were on the porches the conversation stopped while they passed. First the male voices faded and halted, then the lighter voices of the women. It was difficult to talk and watch Crystal walk at the same time. She moved all of a perfect piece, with a kind of wiggly-ankled fluid drive, the light curving against the soft waves of her heavy blonde hair.

Crystal was doing a picture-page on St. Luke's Baptist Church and she wanted to see how it looked at night. She was an excellent photographer except during her artsy-fartsy periods when she photographed scenes through wagon wheels and bicycle wheels and the spray of lawn sprinklers and fountains. Fortunately she usually recovered quickly from an attack of artsy-fartsy photography, poking fun at her own work and asking St. James why he let her get away with it. Of course, he didn't always. Only when he was exhausted or his mind was on something else, or he wished a favor of the twenty-three–year-old Coloradoan who several years ago had hit *The Catherine Call* like a bombshell. Her shockingly lovely face and form had almost paralyzed St. James during the job interview, all of his breath going out of him and none wanting to come back in.

The old church was on Sycamore Drive, six blocks from St. James's house.

They climbed age-hollowed slate steps to the granite slabs of the porch and Crystal said that St. Luke's was the oldest church in Alabama. She said she wished he could see the hand-hewn, arched beams in the sanctuary and he did not tell her that as a reporter some years past he had done exhaustive research on the place and written a long story on its history.

"I don't see why they always lock churches up at night," Crystal said, twisting the knob of a massive door.

St. James said he could think of a half-dozen reasons.

"Hey, it's open," said Crystal, giggling, apparently beginning to feel the drinks.

"So waddaya want to do, kid, go in and pray?"

"No, I want to show you—I know how to turn on the lights."

"Big deal."

"Don't be a squimp."

"What's a squimp?"

"I don't know, come on, let's go in."

She swung open the intricately carved slab of walnut and he followed her inside the foyer and then into the sanctuary with its high-curving ceiling. There were dim yellow night-lights on either side of the baptismal tank high behind the sloping nest of the choir, the podium and pulpit fronting the choir seats.

"You know we're trespassing," St. James whispered, but she tugged at his arm and he found himself timidly following her along the central aisle to the front pews where they sat down and stared silently at the green, glowing water behind a glass plate along the upper edge of the baptismal tank. "Would you like the big lights on?" Crystal giggled. "I know where the switch is."

"No."

"Why not?" She could drink a great deal for an hour or so, without any sign of intoxication. When it caught up with her it came all at once and she could be pretty crazy. One New Year's Eve they stood on the river bridge throwing cherry bombs out over the water. Crystal began holding the powerful, stubby firecrackers between her teeth and lighting them with his Zippo. She could have blown off her nose and God knows what all if he hadn't seized the paper bag of cherry bombs and thrown it in the river.

"You drunk?" he said now.

"Maybe."

"I don't think there's any maybe about it." St. James was getting nervous. "Let's get out of here."

"We're not trespassing," said Crystal. "I'm an honorary member. A holy representative of the goddamned media." Her voice soared eerily in the vaulted silence of the room. The glow of a streetlight lit up a couple of stained-glass windows to the right of the altar. A police car passed, its siren yelping, its rotating lights causing the stained flowers and figures in the windows to leap and flame. He held his breath until the noise faded, the prowl car going west on Sycamore in the cool spring night.

When Crystal arose from the pew he made no move to stop her, his mind still on the police car. He simply sat there, thinking his thoughts, buzzing mildly with beer and bourbon, reassuring himself that the spooky telephone call was the work of Orson Boles. It was too much of a coincidence to be anyone else. Orson making a couple of slingshots. The Little David business. *And he slang it and smote the Philistine in his forehead.* Slang it sounded like Boles—or maybe that's the way it was written in the Bible. Slang and shat and spat and begat and all that. Sometimes, when Orson was riding high with his corn-pone talk, he sounded a great deal like the Bible.

"Come on up," Crystal called to him.

He looked around and didn't see her.

"Up here," she giggled, "I'm in the tank."

He could see her breasts and shoulders and the absurd earrings dimly beyond the glass face of the tank, and her head more clearly above the upper edge of the glass. As his eyes continued to adjust to the gloom she raised an arm high above her head and squealed.

"Godsake, shut up and get out of there," he said, hissing the words.

"Come get me."

"I'm not coming into that thing, Crystal, you fool, get out a there."

"Nope." She commenced splashing the green-black water and he saw silver-green bubbles behind the glass as she vanished.

He sat, transfixed in the polished oaken pew, waiting. In a moment she appeared and began swimming around. There was no other sound than her splashing and his breathing and an occasional snort as she cleared her nose to dive again. He got up and ran along the aisle to the wall separating sanctuary and foyer, finding a wall switch there and flipping it. It lit up the wrong part of the room and he cut it off and tried another switch, and another, until only the altar and tank were illuminated. "Now," he said, approaching the tank, "come on out a there, honey—you don't want to get us in trouble."

"Come get me." Her hair was slicked to her head, so that she looked much smaller, like a wet cat.

He moved up the steps of the sloping choir loft and tried to reach over the glass and grab her, but she moved away from him, laughing softly and sticking out her tongue.

"Crystal, if you don't come out a there I'm going to fire your ass, you hear me?"

"Fire away, boss man."

"I'm not kidding."

"Me neither, boss man. I'm sick of taking pictures of new PTA presidents and Country Club champs and Kiwanians and Rotarians and Civitans and Elks and Shriners. Sick to *death* of it. And I'm sick of you and your foul temper and smugness and vile language."

"Okay stay there—stay there till you shrivel, goddamit."

"I don't shrivel."

"Well, shit, until you melt, I'm getting out of here." But he knew he could not leave her drunk in the baptismal font. She sometimes got so goofy when she drank that she would just as soon drown herself to spite him. She really could do it, just for the hell of it.

He found a door to the left of the tank and pushing aside a heavy beige curtain of monk's cloth he stood in the cove where the preacher entered the tank with his lambs. Crystal back-paddled to the other end of the tank, the crushed-glass eyes laughing up at him. "C'mon in big boy."

"Please, Crystal, don't be crazy tonight."

"Nope."

"You can have the Folsom assignment," he said. She wanted to do a layout on life at the penitentiary and had been badgering him for months.

"Nope." She splashed water at him, wetting the front of his pants.

"You name it," he said, "and you can have it."

"You want me, come get me, it isn't deep. You won't *drown*, you know."

To his amazement he found himself in the tank, moving toward her and then holding her against him. The water was cool, but not uncomfortable. The top of her head was under his chin as he held her and suddenly, the beer and bourbon simmering in his head and chest, enjoying the semi-weightlessness and the feel of her, he felt a great peace, a lessening of apprehension which by degrees left him loose and light in the green water.

Crystal said quietly beneath his chin, her voice coming off the surface of the water and the walls of the tank, "I always wanted to be baptized. In my church in Colorado they just sprinkle you. Sprinkling is so damned stingy, don't you think? Just a little on your hair."

"I guess so." He felt an overpowering sense of sympathy and protectiveness for her. Had he ever been that young? And vulnerable? And nutty?

"Will you baptize me, Kiel?"

"I don't know how, come on honey, let's go home." He tried to steer her toward the steps but she turned inside his arms and was free.

"I'm serious," she said.

"If I baptize you will you come with me?"

"Yes."

He thought he heard the slam of a distant door in the rear of the church. "Okay, I baptize thee in the name of the father, the son and the Holy Ghost. Now for Christsake come on."

"You've got to hold my nose and duck me."

Half walking and half swimming he made his way to her and ducked her, listening for footsteps, putting her under quietly so that he would be able to hear them, but knowing that everything was carpeted and that whoever it was that slammed the door would be on top of them before they heard him.

"*Do* it to me," Crystal breathed.

"What?"

"Do it to me *here*."

"In the tank?"

"Yes, in front of God and *everybody*," said Crystal. She didn't sound drunk, just intently serious.

He reached out and lifted her chin with his left hand and he raised his right arm clear of the water and hit her with the heel of his right hand. He felt the shock of the blow travel up his forearm into his shoulder. Holding onto her he went underwater and hoisted her onto his shoulder, climbed up out of the tank, and made his way drippingly through the sanctuary to the front door. He saw no one as he descended the slate steps carrying Crystal into the shadows on the side of the building.

8

ALFRED DEASON WAS A DAPPER MAN WHO HAD BEEN VERY fat before his coronary but now was built like a dirt-dauber. He was extremely proud of his small waist and went around patting his flat belly as if to reassure himself the bulge was gone for keeps. As president of the Catherine Farmers' Trust he sought to project an image of vast prosperity, although the truth was that a year ago the bank nearly sank because it was spread too broad and thin and could not collect enough from delinquent debtors to satisfy the federal auditors. Deason, who was reared in the rural village of Orion and attended a cow-college in northeastern Alabama, had had to jettison his leased Lear jet and a fifty-foot motor yacht which he kept in the bay at Mobile.

"You look awful tense, Kiel, it don't pay to be tense—that newspaper getting to ya?"

"No more than usual," said St. James, impressed despite himself by a desk the size of a Ping-Pong table. "I guess the stress goes with the territory."

Deason punched a button and spoke into the intercom: "Myra, would you bring us some coffee, dear? Two of us." He lifted his eyebrows at St. James and said, "Cream and sugar? Would you rather have tea or a Coke?"

"Black coffee'll be fine." St. James glanced at his watch. "I don't have long, Al. I wanted to talk to you about C.B."

Deason leaned back into sage-green leather and said, "You see?"

"See what?"

"Hurry-hurry-worry-worry, it don't do a cotton-pickin' bit a good. I learned that the hard way." He opened his blue flannel blazer with the Country Club crest on the pocket and patted his belly with both hands. "You know how I shake that stress-monkey off my back?"

"I really *am* pressed for time, Al."

"I meditate." Deason beamed and rubbed his belly.

"That's good, Al, that's good stuff." St. James hoped fervently that he would not have to hear again about the triple bypass the banker underwent at Houston. Or any of Deason's other surgical sufferings. The last thing in the world St. James wished was one of Deason's organ recitals. Half a lung. Half a colon and the rest of it. Deason discussed them with unseemly relish and at length whenever he could work them into the conversation, which was often.

"I'm told you were perhaps C.B.'s closest friend, Al?"

"When I medi-tate," said Deason, "I lay down and go loose as a goose and you know what I think about?"

"No, Al, I don't. Do you know anyone who might have had it in for the commissioner?"

"*Numbers*," the banker smiled, closing his eyes. "I'm doing it right now. I see a big number one rising up out of a blue lake and I see the foam break as the number comes out of the water. I see it clear as you sitting there in that chair."

St. James sighed and raked at his ear and squinched his eyes shut in irritation.

"And now I see a number *two* sailing up out of the water and the water is so blue it makes you feel funny and the numeral is red as blood and big as a boxcar. All that creamy white foam and the red against a pale blue sky."

"My God, Al, how many numbers *are* there?"

"Keep your britches on and lissen, Kiel. Number three is coming. You can see the water commence to stir and a pinkness underneath and here she *comes*. . . Do you see it, do you see the glow of it under the water?"

"No," said St. James. All he could see with his eyes closed was Crystal in the tank, his hand under her chin just before he knocked her cold and hauled her out of the church. The bruise was slight, but she would say nothing to him when she regained her senses. She would not even look at him during the walk back to the house where she climbed into the Jaguar and burned two ruts in the yard backing out. The powerful little car stalled in the deep gravel of the driveway after spewing plumes of rocks all the way across the street.

"There she blows," said Deason faintly, as if drained by an orgasmic satisfaction, "old number three, coming up . . ."

"I tell you what," said St. James, getting to his feet, his face flushed with frustration and anger. "You can stick old number three up yourself."

Deason opened his eyes and said in a quiet, reasonable voice. "Okay, so C.B. was my friend. I loaned him money to buy a house and a new car now and then. In our drinking days we got drunk together and sometimes we drove over to New Orleans to watch the horses run at the Fair

Grounds. We were drafted together in War Two and served in the same Quartermaster Company. I've eaten dinner with him and Nina and he and Nina've eaten dinner at my place. But I don't have the vaguest idea who'd want to fix his clock."

"Think about it," said St. James, sitting down. "Do you know Dillard and Stephanie Harmon?"

"I've danced with her at the club and Dillard keeps my BMW running. She's just a baby, but stacked. You've seen her."

"Not to my knowledge."

"You'd damned well know if you'd seen her."

"That nice, huh?"

Deason just smiled and leaned deeper into his green leather and massaged his belly.

"Was C.B. involved with her?"

"If you mean was he sleeping with her, I wouldn't know. I know that he wanted to; but then every man at the club had an eye on her. She flirts a lot, but I don't know anybody besides Dillard that's balled her. Y'know some girls that flirt won't take it much farther than that; and some of the quiet, mousy little things that you think butter wouldn't melt in their pussy, they will screw you just as fast as they can draw their ass back."

St. James, recognizing the resounding truth of Deason's observation, said, "How does Dillard take the flirting?"

"He don't like it, would you?"

"I guess not—what I'm saying is do you think he could get jealous enough to become violent."

"To kill?"

"Yes."

"I can't say. I don't know of him laying a hand on anybody except Stephanie. And I didn't see him do that; but somebody blacked both her eyes."

"How long ago was that?"

"Maybe a couple of weeks, I'm not sure. No more than a month."

"She went to the club with a couple of shiners?"

"Naw, I saw her at a garage sale. She was wearing sunglasses, but from the side you could see that somebody popped her pretty good."

"Did she say anything about her eyes."

"No, and I didn't either. I wasn't about to ask her anything about 'em. I figured it was her business." The banker stood up and said he didn't know what happened to the coffee. He took a few steps toward the door of the office, then thrust his hands in his pants pockets and pirouetted on his little shiny feet. "You ought to try my diet, Kiel, no red meat, just chicken and turkey and fish and vegetables, makes the hell of a difference."

St. James got up and sucked in his own gut. He had the mild beginning of a pot. "Your wife cook all that stuff for you, Al, or you have it flown in from Antoine's?"

"Our nigger cooks for us. Had her for years. Shoot, she's just like one a the *family*."

St. James flinched and started to say something ugly. Instead, he said, "Gee, Al, I thought maybe the chicken came busting up out of that fucking blue lake."

The city editor of *The Catherine Call* knew from experience that the best way to reestablish rapport with Crystal was to do something nice for her "critters." So when he left the bank he drove to Delchamps supermarket and bought some cookies and grits for her beaver and a head of lettuce and a tomato for the turtle. He also bought a couple of packets of Meeow for the two cats.

Crystal had picked up the big turtle on the road to Birmingham where someone had run over it in a car or

44

truck and left it bleeding, the hump of its shell crushed. She squirted some kind of mycin stuff into the wound and plastered the broken shell with ready-mix concrete to form a cast, putting the turtle into a washtub which it very nearly filled, and covering it with sawdust. This happened in November when nights were cold so she trained the cats to sleep on top of the sawdust to keep the turtle warm. Not until early March did she remove the creature from the tub, only to find that its hind legs were paralyzed and that it could not fend for itself. Now she kept it in a homemade cage with the beaver in the kitchenette of her small apartment. The beaver was crippled too in one leg and was given to her by a friend in the state Game and Fish Department who rescued it from a trap. The past two weeks the cage had been in the back yard of the apartment complex.

When St. James had fed the beaver and tried to make the turtle eat he fed the cats and left the empty packets of cat food near the beaver cage so Crystal would know he wished to make amends.

At one time or another she had befriended stray dogs, rabbits, and even an injured squirrel. The editor did not like the turtle. It had a cruel mouth and looked as if it would like to bite the hell out of you. The shell had mended but you could still see where it was squashed by a tire of a car or truck. It would eat heartily when Crystal fed it, but when St. James dropped leaves of lettuce and pieces of tomato into the beaver cage the turtle simply gazed at the stuff with those cold, dusty eyes.

Crystal said sometimes the turtle, whose name was Sutter, tried to bite her, and that she kept it not so much because she felt affection for it, but because she knew the turtle was her responsibility. She said it was no accident that she saw it on the highway. She believed firmly in a

Great Design, but could not, or would not, explain the nature of it. Drunk or sober she declined to talk much about it.

It was not unlikely she felt that St. James was destined to have sex with her in the baptismal tank, and that he had violated the Design. His feeling was that if he had done it God would have whacked him good, one way or another.

9

ROBERT GOODBEE BREATHED THROUGH A HOLE IN HIS chest and when he coughed he coughed through the hole, which was covered loosely with filthy tape and a red flannel rag of the kind used to wipe grease off engines in commercial garages. Some kind of malignancy and subsequent surgery had destroyed his esophagus and nasal passages and he could not talk.

Now he wrote on a notebook St. James handed him: IF YOU'RE ASKING DID I SEE MR. BARRINGTON OUT HERE THE DAY OF THE KILLING, THE ANSER IS NO.

Goodbee sat in a homemade rocker which still had tree bark on it in places. The back and seat were covered with cowhide which had clotted, dried blood on one side and brown-and-white fur on the other. The half-cured hide added to the symphony of smells in the small single room of the shanty on the southern edge of the dump. The room was filthy and Goodbee's writing hand was so gummy that when he tried to return the pencil to the editor it stuck to blackened claws.

"You keep it, sir," St. James said hastily. "Keep the notebook, too, you may need them."

Boles had tried to interrogate Goodbee soon after the murder, but met with little success. The detective said Goodbee was seldom home and resented intruders, that he picked up a stick and chased off three ladies from the Church of Our Lord Jesus Christ who brought him a food basket and household supplies.

Goodbee now printed in capital letters: YOU GOT A CIGARETTE?

St. James said no, that he had quit smoking six weeks ago and was chewing.

TEN I'LL HAVE TO SMOKE MY OWN. WILL YOU LITE IT FOR ME?

St. James lit the Picayune cigarette and handed it to Goodbee who grinned and lifted the flannel rag over the hole in his chest. The hole was making a whistling sound as Goodbee stuck the tip of the cigarette in it and took a deep drag, blowing the smoke out in a pencil-thin plume. St. James saw the angry redness of the hole and averted his eyes and as he did so Goodbee began coughing through the hole in his chest, a wet, terrifying sound.

"You really shouldn't smoke, sir," said St. James, walking to an open window for air. There was a coal oil stove near the window, some meat and onions bubbling in a wash pail. It looked like three or four squirrels simmering in brown gravy. "Your dinner smells nice," he said. "You must be a good cook."

Goodbee nodded, looking pleased.

"Where'd you get the squirrels?"

THEM AINT SQUIRREL.

"Oh?"

THEM'S RATS.

"Well," said St. James queasily. "They smell nice. If

they had bushy tails they would look just like squirrels, wouldn't they? Skinned, you can't tell a difference."

I LIKE YOU, Goodbee printed on the pad. YOU OKAY. Suddenly he seemed quite taken with the editor. THEY ABOUT READY TO EAT NOW, I GOT A LOAF A NEW BRED.

"I thank you, sir, for your hospitality, but I have bleeding ulcers. Baby food in jars is all I can keep down." St. James returned to the window, placing both hands on the sill and raising his shoulders, breathing deeply. The total disaster of the old man's life and his eagerness to share his food, to share what little he had. It was too much. Robert Goodbee's lot in life made the sufferings of Job seem nothing worse than a light case of poison ivy. But God he stank. Every time he waved the notebook and St. James returned to him to read a message it was nauseating. Why can't you bathe, you heartbreaking old sonofabitch? If I break down, will you laugh? Can you laugh through that hole?

St. James turned from the window, knowing that he could not and would not stand any more of this and saying, "Well, if you see anything suspicious around here, maybe you'll get word to me."

Goodbee nodded, rising with difficulty from the rocker and going to the stove to stir the stew. He clacked the spoon against the inside of the pot to get the gravy off of it and wiped it on the red rag on his chest. The clutter in the room was incredible. Cans filled with rusted nails and nuts and bolts. The wheel and torn tire of a motorbike. A strangely new yellow crutch on the floor beside the filthy bed with its naked, stained mattress. There was no table. Everything was on the floor, rocks and sticks and what appeared to be the thighbone of a cow or horse, a canful of dried peach seed, one can half-filled with tacks, a crumpled mosquito bar in a corner, a soiled and rippled Confederate flag, drifts and piles of barely identifiable or completely mysterious rubbish in the corners and along the base of the walls which were papered with ancient pages of *The Catherine Call*. One time-scorched page carried the attack on Pearl Harbor, another the story of Christiaan Barnard's first heart transplant. There were more recent headlines on test shafts and tunnels at Pimm, which was north of Catherine, a site still under consideration as a nuclear-waste storage complex.

As he prepared to leave, St. James glanced down at a large tomato can filled with crystalline kids' playing marbles. Lying on top the clear green marbles was a slingshot made of wood and steel and surgical tubing. The translucent tubing dangled over the edge of the can, its leather rock-pocket resting on the floor. St. James stooped and picked up the slingshot, his heart racing and Goodbee made a whistling, wet noise and lifted his hand in protest. He hobbled to St. James, bringing pad and pencil with him. THAT THERE'S MY GRANDSON'S.

"Why did he leave it here?" St. James asked, looking directly into Goodbee's eyes.

HE WAS SHOOTING SOME RATS FOR ME.

"Well, sir, he must be a pretty fair shot, heh?"

HE MISSES A LOT.

St. James examined the slingshot. The rubber tubing was fitted over forks of steel, the metal running through channels on both sides and bottom of the wooden handle. Holding the handle in his right fist and extending the right arm St. James pulled the empty rock-pocket back until it almost touched his chin. When he released it the pocket snapped forward in a blur and cracked painfully against the back of the right hand. "Pretty powerful weapon," he said, grimacing, rubbing the back of his hand. "Wouldn't you say?"

HE SHOOTS THEM MARBLES IN IT. THEY KNOCK A RAT SILLY.

St. James loaded the pocket with a marble and stepped out the front door which was level with the earth. He pulled the rubber back until he feared it would snap, then released it and the marble vanished, a melting, whizzing speck against a cotton-wool sky.

When the newspaperman returned to the room, Goodbee stood waiting for him with a single-shot .410-gauge shotgun. The clean smell of gun oil was sharp in the stench of the room.

"What's the matter?" said St. James. "Put that thing down."

Goodbee held the small gun against his shoulder with one hand, a finger inside the trigger-guard. He beckoned for St. James to give him the slingshot. There was no mistaking the hand signal and the look in the brown eyes. St. James surrendered the slingshot and as he did so he stared at the finger which appeared to be curling against the trigger of the .410.

When Goodbee had the slingshot he waggled the gun at the door and it was clear that the interview was ended.

"I thought we were buddies, Mr. Goodbee."

Another wave of the gun. A whistling of the chest, the flannel rag blowing outward. Smell of gravy and onions. Whiff of an awful interlacing of nightmare odors in this tragedy of squalor and decay. Goodbee dropped the slingshot and leveled the shotgun and that was that.

Boles said that as far as he knew Robert Goodbee had no record of violence and that he doubted the man could stretch the rubber of a slingshot far enough to kill anything much larger than the rats he ate. "He used to be a sawyer back in the days when the land around here was virgin piney woods. Sawyer's job is sharpening saws. He made good money because the work requires skill, a specialized skill. I'm talking about the big ripsaws and band saws and the crosscut jobs, not little household or carpentering saws."

"What brought him down?" said St. James.

"I don't know, hoss, but down he is. I know that he draws food stamps and don't have to eat rats. And he has Social Security and a pension as a disabled veteran. His shack is on city property and the city knows it but don't levy any taxes on it. How can you tax a mess like that?"

Boles was very much interested in the slingshot and said that he planned to seize it as evidence in the Barrington case if Goodbee refused to hand it over. "You done some good work today, hoss, maybe it ain't true what they say about you."

"And what's that?"

"That you done lost ya zing, you over the hill. Too many beers. Too many deadlines. You going to jog with me Sunday?"

Almost every Sunday that the weather was good they met at the City Park Zoo and jogged in a loop westward around the college tennis courts and back. It wasn't true jogging, but rather a compromise between jogging and walking. Boles called it "wogging" when he was feeling cute.

"I'll be there," said St. James, dreading it.

"Same place?"

"Yep, I'll see you at the baboon cage."

"Fine, I hope them apes have growed some hair on their ass. It's hard to take early in the morning, all them raw, purple asses smeared with that white stuff. Do baboons shit white?"

"I don't know and I don't *want* to know."

"Maybe the SPCA smears zinc oxide ointment on'em."

"Do you enjoy making me sick at my stomach, Orson?

I'm sick to death of you talking about the goddamned baboons. Did you ever finish making your two sling-shots?"

Boles said he had indeed; and that he would bring them with him Sunday and they could test them then. He said he would show them to St. James now, but they were in a desk drawer at home. Then: "I'm thinking about sponsoring a competition for people who like to sling rocks. Waddaya think of that, hoss?"

"I think it's a clever idea."

Boyes grinned, tapping his temple. "Thinking, hoss, always thinking. I can't believe you didn't get the name of Goodbee's grandson. If he's *got* a grandson."

"You talked to the old man. I'd say I learned a hell of a lot more than you did, Ironsides."

"Okay, okay, you don't have to get in a squiff m'boy. This here investigation's only *begun*."

It rained hard all that night, and the following day, Sunday, it continued to pour. St. James was delighted. It meant that he did not have to meet Boles for the weekly stint of exercise; so he made himself a pot of very black coffee and after a couple of cups he sat on his front porch and chewed tobacco, sitting in the old chair with the slingback and spitting over the edge of the porch into the swamp of the yard. Boles claimed there were two kinds of chewing tobacco, *parlor* tobacco and *field* to-bacco. The newspaperman had found plenty of the squirty kind for outdoor use, but as yet had been unable to locate the parlor stuff, which Boles said required only minimal spitting.

Hundreds of thousands of acorns from the oaks border-ing the property floated in the rainwater and when he spit into a floating island of acorns it broke apart and came back together. But after a time he grew bored and went into the empty house and looked up Dillard Harmon's phone number and dialled it.

He had no clear-cut plan beyond a desire to talk again to the mechanic and to observe him and his wife together and possibly to ask Stephanie Harmon a few questions. This time he would try to be less irritating and awkward and really seek to learn something about the couple's feelings toward the dead city commissioner. Perhaps it would come to nothing, but it seemed worth trying, certainly more rewarding than spitting off the porch. The cigarette craving was heavy upon him and although the chewing brought minor relief it did not attend entirely to his need.

Stephanie answered the phone and he asked to speak to her husband.

"He's at work," said Stephanie. "One a the garbage trucks broke down and he's trying to get it rolling for Monday."

"Mrs. Harmon, would you mind if I came by for a time and talked with you."

"About what? Who are you?"

"Oh, I'm sorry, I'm Kiel St. James. I'm city editor of *The Catherine Call.*"

"My sakes *alive*," she said in a teasing voice. "What do you want to talk about?"

"I'd rather tell you when I get there." He did not want to turn her off on the telephone, without even getting a chance to interrogate her.

"I don't have on any *clothes*," she said.

"Oh that's all right."

She giggled, then broke into genuine laughter. "I'll just *bet* it is."

"I mean I won't be there for thirty minutes or so, and you'll have plenty of time."

54

"You disappoint me." Still teasingly, now openly provocative.

"Can I come?"

"I don't know, *can* you?"

"I'll be there," he said, looking at his watch. "About ten o'clock."

"Okay," said Stephanie Harmon, "I'll be waiting for you."

As he headed for the front door the phone rang and he was almost certain it would be Stephanie, that she had called Dillard and her husband said no soap. But it turned out to be Boles, who said maybe St. James would like to drop by his house and look at the slingshots. "I did a fair job if I do say so myself, newshound."

St. James lied unnecessarily, saying that the owners of the paper had scheduled another seminar for this morning, a snap decision on the part of SNA, and that he had no choice but to attend. The Southeastern Newspaper Alliance, which had bought the newspaper from the Holifield cousins of Birmingham, loved seminars, St. James told Boles. This much was true.

"Hoss, you spend half your time in them seminars. What's this one about—emergency pussy for single men?"

"Yes," said St. James, "but you got to be able to prove it's an emergency, Orson."

"Waddaya have to do, hang a couple a Holiday Inn bathtowels on it?"

"Just one, Orson, they are not unreasonable people when you get to know them."

10

STEPHANIE HARMON WAS A BIG GIRL, ALMOST AS TALL AS St. James. Her hair was a thick clean flame which whirled about her face in one of those every-whichaway coiffures popularized some years back by Farrah Fawcett. The red hair was for real and looked nothing like the stuff women buy in bottles or in the beautician's chair. She was barefoot and wore black Vietcong-type pajamas.

"You cert'ny took your time," she smiled, taking him by the arm and leading him to a couch long enough to accommodate Kareem Abdul-Jabbar.

He glanced at his watch. "I'm sorry."

She sat beside him, her red-nailed hands very white against the black knees of the pajamas, back straight, full breasts tight against the cloth. She appeared about the same age as Crystal, perhaps twenty-two. "Can I fix you a drink?"

"That would be nice."

"I love to drink when it's raining, don't you?"

"Sure." The couch was extremely soft and springy and

56

he felt an abrupt need to loosen his necktie and unbutton the collar of his shirt.

"Wild Turkey or Smirnoff's?" She polished her lips with the tip of her tongue and smiled as if they had a secret of some sort between them.

"The bourbon will be fine."

"I just knew you were goin' to say that," she said, making a complete slow turn on the balls of the pretty feet. Probably something she picked up competing for queen of the district livestock show. She really was about as phony and corny as they came, but after a time you didn't much care. He felt a kind of humming from her and it began to fill his chest and belly and adjacent areas. He remembered how catty Nina had been, the stuff about Stephanie being the nineteenth hole at the Country Club. *She's in heat. I mean seven days a week. Anybody. Everybody.* Nina could have been simply jealous. She was beginning to wilt around the edges. Stephanie, tacky or not, was in full bloom, fresh flesh, smoky green eyes, very little makeup, the long-legged boneless look of natural young beauty.

St. James played the game despite a feeling of embarrassment. "How'd you know I wanted bourbon, Miz Harmon?"

"You have that *look*."

"The bourbon look?"

"You know, cowboys and stuff. Do you want to spit out that tobacco? I can get you an empty coffee can from the kitchen, that's what Dillard uses."

"Please." He'd completely forgotten the cud; but it didn't appear to repel her. Maybe she doted on brown corners.

She brought him the can and a glass of water to swish his mouth clean and soon she returned with the drinks,

57

two bourbons on ice in chunky glasses which were frosted. He took a sip and made a happy face as she eased in beside him on the super-couch. He felt her breast sliding against his elbow and heard her breathing, then felt her hand on him and her lips against the side of his neck.

And he thought, *Good God A'mighty, Nina was right.* Instant intercourse. The awful thing about it was that he was as ready for her as if there had been an hour of foreplay. He could see himself on top of her hammering it for all it was worth and her husband coming up behind him and beating his brains to paste with that open-end wrench.

"I wanted to ask you . . ."

"It can wait," she breathed into his mouth. "Oh God, I want you, I want you *inside* me *now*."

She squirmed around, still kissing him, almost gagging him with a tongue of remarkable length and dexterity, and somehow she shucked off the black cotton pajama pants without missing a lick. She seemed to be counting his teeth with her tongue, then probing in an absurdly businesslike manner, then flipping the tongue from side to side. Amusement came to his aid; in all his years and travels he had never tried tongue-wrestling.

When she pulled her tongue out of his mouth, it sounded like somebody jerking a stick out of the mud. "Don't you want *me?*" she gasped, falling back beside him, her face white, jaws open, panting at the ceiling.

"You're married, ma'am," St. James said idiotically. He could not think of anything else to say and desire for her had been snuffed by the foolishness of her.

"You had it *up*," she said. "You had it *up*, what happened to it?"

"I dunno."

Her hand was on him. "Are you queer?"

"Not as I know, Miz Harmon."

"Well, it seems to me you'd be the *first* to know. I swear if I don't believe all the men are pansies anymore, or they got herpes or something. I had ahold of it and everything was going fine and it just melted in my hand."

"Yes ma'am."

"Did you come?"

"Well, ma'am," said St. James, trying not to grin at the absurdity of the situation. "I'm *here* so I must've come."

"You know what I mean, you crazy jackass." As she fumed she was getting back into her pants. She was able to do it in no time at all. "What do you *want* anyway?"

"I wanted to know if there was anything between you and C.B. Barrington."

"Just about as much as there is between you and me."

"I'm sorry, I'm really sorry. Did you ever hear your husband threaten Mr. Barrington? I mean did he happen to come across the two of you in a compromising situation?"

"Not hardly, now git outa here."

"I know you're put out with me, Miz Harmon, but just bear with me a minute. Did Dillard have any reason to want to hurt C.B.?"

"No." She had regained both her pants and her composure and now she lit a cigarette which she plucked from a Chinesey-looking box on a cocktail table near the couch. "Y'know, I'm rilly dis-a-pointed in you, Mr. St. James."

"Was your husband working the morning of the killing or was he here with you?"

"He was here sleeping off a hangover, a real woolly booger. We partied all night long. He's a real man, Dillard is." She had begun whining, meowing like the talking cats on the cat food commercials. "I don't know why I fool *around* the way I do."

"Would you swear under oath that Dillard was with you?"

"You git," said Stephanie. "You git right this minute and don't let the door hit you in the behind."

It seemed to him he never left a place of his own volition anymore. Goodbee. Crystal. Both the Harmons. Everybody disgruntled or worse. Much of it was ludicrous; nevertheless, he was beginning to feel unwanted.

What he had intended to do with Stephanie was to ask questions about her stormy relationship with Dillard, to gain her confidence with his sympathy—something he would not have to feign—and hope that she would open up with helpful facts about the Barrington business.

Stephanie diverted him, melted first his brain, then his erection. *Would you swear under oath that Dillard was with you?* Had he really asked that? Cranking up the gray Honda Civic hatchback St. James felt the slow blush spreading. What did Mark Twain say? Something about people are the only animals that blush—or need to?

"Ridiculous," he said to his eyes in the rear-view mirror. "You are ridiculous."

He didn't expect to find Crystal at the newspaper on Sunday; but since she still wasn't talking to him, it didn't matter. There was a pile of unopened mail on his desk and he went to work on it. A big box from SNA contained T-shirts commemorating the staff's coverage of a major flood several months past The Southeastern Newspaper Alliance's executive vice-president had tucked a brief note in with the T-shirts commending the "energy and imagination" of the staff in "an extreme emergency." Printed on the chest of each T-shirt was:

WE COVERED THE 1984 FLOOD
And we did it well.

This was SNA's idea of a morale-builder, a motivational

strategy of genuine impact. On one occasion they sent scarlet and blue and white baseball caps with a silver whirlwind enbroidered on them, commemorating coverage of a tornado at Pimm. Elwood, the general manager of *The Catherine Call,* wore his cap on weekends when he dropped by the newspaper on real or imagined business; and he no doubt would wear his T-shirt although he never even wet his wingtips in the flood. He appeared disappointed in those who declined to wear the caps. St. James was in this group.

St. James dumped the box of shirts on Barney's desk in sports. Barney loved his cap and so did the members of his team. He and the others all were young and full of piss and vinegar and they wore things even funnier than the caps and shirts.

"Truce," said Crystal, slapping his desk to get his attention.

"I didn't know there was a war," he said, feeling ridiculously pleased that she wanted to talk to him. Since he had hit her in the tank at the church she'd spoken only when it was necessary in responding to orders or requests.

"Oh yes." There was laughter in her voice but she was not smiling. "Didn't you know I was mad at you?"

"No," he lied. "I really didn't notice it kid, what riled you?"

"The truth's not in you, boss. Sometimes it won't even come near you."

"Okay, so what now?"

"What would you like?"

"I don't know, I never know." He pulled a frown and sought to look worldly—the gruff, disenchanted foreman of the newsroom.

"Someone tells me that John Trask, who owns the Honda sales agency, is a crony of Dillard Harmon. Did you know that?"

61

"Who told you about Harmon?"

"That's not important," Crystal said, reaching across his desk to lay her hand on his. "I just thought you might want to know; if you'd rather, I'll put Orson Boles on it."

"I'd rather you didn't."

"Would you like a ride in the country? With the top down on the Jag? We can stick our tongues out in the rain."

"I'd like that," St. James said. "But don't mention tongues to me. I think I'm off them."

"For keeps?"

"Are you crazy?"

"Good," said Crystal. "I couldn't bear it. I mean a man permanently finished with tongues is a poor man, indeed." Crystal remained deadpan, but she lifted her left shoulder and turned her head to look at him out the sides of her eyes and it was beginning to seem like old times. She was wearing a tank top, and the bare shoulder under the chin always got to him. If she'd done that at the church he probably would have taken her right there in the tank.

"Well," said Crystal, "shall we take that ride? We don't absolutely *have* to stick out our tongues."

"Fine," he said. But it was not to be.

The police-and-fire radio scanner crackled and came to life on Brenda Keeton's desk. Triple-A Ambulance Service was en route to an accident at the intersection of Oak and Maple. A young mother on a bicycle with her baby in one of those kiddy seats behind her had lost control when the kid caught his bare foot in the rear wheel. The police radio dispatcher said in his normal voice: "Spokes ripped off the baby's toes just before she whacked into the side of a van."

St. James said to Crystal: "You better get out there kid and see what there is to see. Try to get a shot of the crumpled bike, we can't use the baby's foot—maybe you'll beat the meat-wagon there and shoot them loading the people into the ambulance."

By the time he finished his unnecessary instructions Crystal was going out the front door with her camera.

When she was gone he sat motionless for a time, not touching the stacked mail, trying to make his mind a blank. Trying to wrench his thoughts away from the small, torn foot in the meat-eating spokes of the wheel.

Why didn't he get away from all this?

Surely he had paid his dues with a quarter-century of blood and guts, killings, rapes, tornadoes and hurricanes, political horseshit, grassfires, factory fires, train wrecks, and trying to make sense of the stuff, much of it handwritten, from country correspondents, the stringers. Antebellum recipes for tea cookies. Church socials. Terse accounts of rural domestic tragedy: "Amos Tewkes, who stepped on a ham can in his yard, died Thursday of blood poisoning at his first cousin's home on RFD 3. . . . Mr. Tewkes' wife, the former Mary Alice Roberts, was killed by a cow seven years ago. . . ." Most of the stringers were very old and had worked many years for *The Catherine Call*. Some of them mailed in their "strings"—the clippings of their stories they pasted end to end since they were paid by the inch. Others delivered them personally, always when St. James was at his busiest. One lady of eighty-four drove her Oldsmobile thirty miles to the newspaper. It was a hair-raising thing to see her pull out of the newspaper parking lot into traffic. "Lorene, someday you going to get run over," St. James chided her. She winked at him and said, "Young man, you can choke to death on a chicken bone at Sunday dinner with all your family around you ten miles from traffic. You can stroke out in a rocking chair. Or you can just plump yourself down in bed and rot. Who wants to rot?"

63

It was a good question.

But there were times that he thought that's what he was doing on this small-town daily. One of his cousins was a senior editor on *U.S. News & World Report*. A friend had a cush job at *Life*. A schoolmate had done well with *The New Yorker*. Some years ago he himself was doing well with the International Wire Service, working as night editor in New Orleans and later at Denver. He was bucking for bureau chief and his personal file was crammed with glowing accounts of his work. But he lacked reverence for the system and the perpetrators thereof and in the end it brought him down—in combination with a vulgar paragraph he tacked onto the end of a story about the dedication of a railroad company's "hump yard."

Ah well, it all came out even at the end.

Barrington could attest to that and God knows the politician had kissed just about every ass in Alabama.

11

IT WAS LATE AFTERNOON WHEN ST. JAMES REACHED HIS
house on Timothy Lane and from the yard he could hear
the phone ringing.

He willed himself not to hurry. Taking his time, he
strolled to the porch and placed a leisurely key in the
lock. Not hurrying was a part of his quitting-smoking
program. A slower pace. Fresh oxygen in the lungs and a
much slower pace. Less food. The first week he had eaten
like an insane hog.

Before he picked up the phone he sensed the voice at
the other end.

The voice, guttural and muffled, said: *"And he took
his staff in his hand and chose him five smooth stones out
of the brook, and put them in a shepherd's bag which he
had, even in a script; and his sling was in his hand; and
he drew near to the Philistine."*

St. James, straining to identify the timbre of the voice,
said, "Stuff it, Bub."

*"And the Philistine came on and drew near to David;
and the man that bare the shield went before . . ."*

A silence then and wheezing at the other end of the line, at times almost a whistling. Then the voice, the words understandable, but less than distinct, measured and heavy. *"And when the Philistine looked about and saw David, he disdained him; for he was but a youth, and ruddy and of a fair countenance."*

St. James, despite himself, felt his belly tightening and he looked about him in the empty bedroom, glancing at the doors as if he expected the owner of the voice to appear, complete with shepherd's sack, whatever the hell that was, smooth stones, staff and sling. If you thought about it, David was pretty flaky. Saul had offered him the royal armor and sword.

"What's your name?" St. James whispered into the phone.

"And the Philistine said unto David, Am I a dog, that thou comest to me with staves? And the Philistine cursed David by his Gods."

Now a protracted spell of the wheezing, a brief coughing fit: *"And the Philistine said to David, come to me and I will give thy flesh to the fowls of the air, and to the beasts of the field."*

St. James laughed—but felt the goose-bumps rising inside his arms. "And I will give thy ass to the cops when I find out who you are, you loony bastard."

"Then said David to the Philistine . . ."

St. James slammed the telephone into its cradle.

Crystal came over that evening, still wearing the yellow tank-top and jeans and western boots, and they ate some of his homemade chili and drank a couple of beers. Crystal's shoulders *breathed*. They seemed to have a life of their own and when they were uncovered they looked nakeder than other shoulders. Everything about her was so fresh, so completely alive, and today it made him feel a thousand years old.

He conveyed this gloomy information to her and she appeared to ponder it with a mouthful of chili. "You're only as old as you feel," she said finally, disappointing him. He expected better from her and usually got it, for her mind was as fresh and keen as her body.

"The ultimate cliche," he said, breaking a fistful of fresh soda crackers into his bowl, stirring them with his spoon.

"No," she said, giving him the sideways thing with the eyes and naked shoulder. "I mean you're only as old as you feel *inside* me."

"Oh."

"Yes, oh, indeed."

"And how old is that?"

She ladled another smoking spoonful of chili and looked at it, but did not eat it. "I'm not sure, Kiel, it's been such a long time—but as I remember, the last time you were inside me you felt about nineteen, maybe twenty."

"That's pretty good."

"And the second time that night, if I recall, you felt maybe forty."

"What about the third time?"

"There was no third time. You tried, but it was like trying to put an oyster in a piggy bank."

"I resent that."

"I did, too," said Crystal.

Later that night he sought to make it up to her and then they talked for a time about the Barrington murder and he told her of the phone call and said that Boles wasn't lying, it couldn't be Boles. "He would have had to call me hoss somewhere in the conversation. His record for not calling me hoss is about thirty seconds."

67

"Are you sure Little David isn't Orson? I mean really sure?"

"Almost," said St. James. "It's all so lopsided, the whole thing. I can't for the life of me understand how Boles can discount the rock being fired from some kind of gun. The traces of gunpowder found on the stone have to mean *something*."

He told her at length about his visits with Goodbee and with Stephanie Harmon, the tongue-wrestler. He did not realize until he was well into that of the tongue that it was a stupid thing to tell Crystal; but Crystal merely looked thoughtful. Soon afterward she said she had to go home and feed the beaver.

When Crystal was gone he returned to the kitchen and had another beer and his third bowl of chili, knowing that he shouldn't—that when he stuffed himself he was inclined to think more kindly of cigarettes. God, but he wanted a Kool Filter King. He was the only white man he knew that smoked Kools. Boles said this was further evidence of his tastes. "It don't matter a whit to you, hoss, who the underdog is—no sir, you going to dig into the heap and get down there with him and *bleed*." Boles loved to irritate him with outrageously racist jokes, and no doubt hoped that Barrington's killer turned out to be a black. In any murder investigation the captain of detectives seemed to interrogate two blacks to one white. Yet he had worked night and day for three weeks to locate and put the collar on a white soybean farmer who raped a sixteen-year-old black girl and had stayed with it until the farmer pleaded guilty and drew a twenty-year hitch at Folsom. The detective was a squirming puzzle of contradictions, a kooky jigsaw which seldom came together in anything resembling a satisfying picture. He would risk his life getting a crazy girl off the roof of a two-story house. And when the family tried to thank him he would say, "Aw shit," and jump in his car, burning rubber to get away from them. He held a Master's Degree in criminal justice and graduated at the top of his class at the FBI's auxiliary school for local and regional law-enforcement officers. Sometimes when he talked he sounded like a redneck, the choice of words, the inflections and colloquialisms pure grits and redeye gravy. On other occasions he sounded as polished and smooth as a university president.

St. James belched chili and beer. It was a super-belch, more a quack, or the cracking of dry wood. He dropped his spoon into the empty bowl and took it to the sink. The sink was loaded with dirty dishes. Crystal usually washed them and he dried while they talked. He'd made a serious mistake telling her about Stephanie's powerful tongue.

What did he truly feel for Crystal? He recognized his need for her, but had small luck in identifying his feelings. It seemed to him that whatever he had for her was more than lust, but less than love, whatever *that* was. How could you be in love with someone who hadn't even been born when you got your first newspaper job? There was something about the blend of vulnerability and cheekiness, the way she turned her head, one minute wild and the next almost timid, the texture and feel of her, everything so tight and right, so damned delicious to be with. Since his divorce several years ago from a good-looking drunk, a professional southern belle, St. James had slept with a number of women. Most of it was very much the same, the absurd posturing and patent lies, pretending that the business of sexual intercourse was much more than it was. You could not pretend with Crystal. Despite her youth she was remarkably allergic to anything that smelled of superficiality or romantic strategy. Sometimes it was depressing. She refused to feign amusement, joy, agreement on a point of argument, or even orgasm. If you failed to get the job done, you knew it with Crystal. His wife May was just the opposite; appearances meant much to her. During sex she flailed about, heels high, panting. Yet he suspected that May had never known genuine orgasm. Nor compassion for that matter.

Standing at the kitchen sink he commenced laughing, trying to imagine May feeding lettuce to a turtle.

He soaked for almost a half hour in a tub of hot water filled with the lather he worked up on his head. Holding his nose he slid down in the tub so that head and face were submerged while he used his free hand to massage his scalp. Ordinarily he enjoyed his underwater ritual, but tonight he kept thinking suppose if Little David crept into the bathroom and did him the dirties. After all, who could say? If Little David was as loony as he sounded he might just bring in the pruning shears from the nail on the back porch and snip off his penis. Maybe a finger or two for good measure.

St. James surfaced much sooner than was his wont. He dried himself hurriedly, acutely aware of the darkness in the hall and the rest of the house. There was a faint glow of light from his bedroom where he had turned on the bedside lamp. Or had he? Was there supposed to be a light on in his room?

He tiptoed to the room, turning on lights as he moved. He looked in his clothes closet and, sheepishly, got down on all fours to peer under the bed. Three dust-balls, and nothing unexpected in the closet either.

He checked the front and back doors and the door of his room, which opened onto a tiny porch where he kept half-used buckets of paint left over from abortive efforts to brighten up the seventy-year-old bungalow. Lights were on next door and he was grateful for the fact that the place now was occupied after years of sitting there empty and rotting. Only last week two men in their thirties had moved into the brick house and sometimes at three o'clock in the morning he could hear them hammering away, trying to make the place livable. They also worked long hours in the yard, planting boxwood and even a pink dogwood tree. They dressed immaculately in shorts that were very short and snug crimson T-shirts and too-white sneakers. Across the street the Siemsens had their lights on late most of the time. Gus Siemsen was a handsome forty-five-year-old orthopedic surgeon with a handsome picture-book family, a lissome well-built wife, and six lissome well-built daughters. Next door to the Siemsens in an almost identical two-storied house of brick was old Mrs. Stevens who occasionally appeared in her yard supported by one of those tubular aluminum walkers. She rented her upstairs to a young couple who owned a Corvette and a yellow dog that looked like a pit bull and in the afternoons the young man would wrap his arms with rags and cuff the dog around until it began snarling and biting. Then he would kneel and speak in low tones to the dog, petting it and scratching its ears until its tail began wagging.

The neighborhood was beautiful this time of year, all the azaleas exploding into incredibly lovely, short-lived blooms which succumbed to the first really rough April storms, the rain hammering the flowers off the stems. The all-day rain today had not helped the azaleas; but somehow it intensified the yummy smell of wisteria and honeysuckle. He hated to block off the fragrances but nevertheless before he retired he locked all three bedroom windows and drew the shades. And he slipped his old .38 Smith & Wesson into a white athletic sock and laid it on the barstool he used as a bedside table. He didn't want the gun to *look* like a gun. Besides, the sock on the stool fit in nicely with the soiled socks and assorted shoes on the floor.

Lying in darkness he listened for sounds in the house. The door was closed between his room and the middle bedroom. Beyond the middle bedroom was the bathroom, then May's old room up front adjacent to the big living-room which she had painted a juicy Edgar Allen Poe scarlet. She must have been drunk when she selected the color; and for a fact she was drunk when she rolled the paint on the walls. The only time she appeared anywhere near happy was when she was painting something or tacking fresh upholstery on a chair, or cleaning the kitchen stove. Every other day she would remove the grills from all four burners, take the white-enameled lid off the stove, and remove the burners. She would boil out the burners in a bucket on the gas heater in the breakfast room. While the burners were boiling in Clorox-water she would mop the linoleum floor in the kitchen. On the rare days, maybe two in a month, that she wasn't riding high on Smirnoff's or Taaka, she simply lay in bed and read murder mysteries. She would sometimes read on through the night. On these occasions she slept until afternoon and resumed the drinking and mopping and the rest of it. She never stumbled around when she drank, and except for the slurred speech and instant hostility she seemed normal. But she did not keep herself as clean as she did the kitchen. The wisteria's perfume had small chance against that of May.

Lying now in his bed, both ears clear of the pillow as he listened for noises, he recalled that May said he worried too much. "If you don't have something to worry about, you *find* something," she said.

And it was the truth.

He could be driving alone down a pretty road, the car humming nicely, nothing hanging over him, no pressure at all, and he would commence fretting about the fact there weren't enough local features in the paper. Or he imagined an incipient toothache or difficulty in swallowing, or worried about whether he'd left the gas on under the coffeepot.

So the hell with it, go to sleep, you stupid bastard. Don't lie here like a frightened girl in your own bed.

He had no solid logic for connecting the voice on the telephone with the weird slaying of C.B. Barrington— beyond the fact the voice appeared obsessed with the David and Goliath thing. And why for Godsake would the killer, if it were the killer, turn his attention to St. James? Did he know that the editor had been trying, with consummate clumsiness and appallingly asinine questions, to help Orson Boles in the investigation? So who knew of the blunderings of Dickless Tracy? Boles? Goodbee? Brenda Keeton and the entire news staff of *The Catherine Call*? Everygoddambody in Catherine?

Go to sleep, he told himself, just roll over and go to sleep. Count boogermen jumping a fence. He thought of Robert Goodbee jumping a fence and whistling through the hole in his chest, the red flannel rag flapping in the rainy wind. Goodbee couldn't jump a footstool. He seemed to have trouble just hobbling across his filthy, cluttered nightmare of a room. What about his mysterious grandson? Boles said as far as he could learn Goodbee had no grandson, only a daughter who lived near the Fairgrounds in New Orleans who came to Alabama once or twice a year and took her father home with her to clean the crud off him and feed him some proper food. Boles said that when she brought the old man back— he refused to live with her—he was dressed decently and looked downright presentable for about a week.

Why had Goodbee seemed so agitated when the sling-shot was plucked from the can?

And why did Dillard Harmon get his ass in an uproar, when all he had to do was shoo St. James off the premises? After all, the man had work to do.

Where was the investigation headed, if indeed it was headed anywhere at all?

Was the killer long gone? A stranger who killed simply for the hell of it? Or who had accidentally plunked the stone squarely between the unfortunate eyes of the commissioner, who happened to turn up at the wrong place at precisely the worst possible time?

Okay, enough of this. The longer you lie awake the more you'll want that cigarette. You hear me? Why don't you get your butt in the car and go to Delchamps and buy five cartons of Kools and smoke every frigging one of them before you have to go to work in the morning? His lungs screamed for smoke. You simply could not chew the monkey off your back. Your lungs got none of the juice.

Around two he fell finally into troubled sleep. He dreamed that Goodbee was wearing striped morning trousers and shiny black shoes and spats—but no shirt. His chest-rag was gone and he looked clean. He stuck his thumb in the hole and honked like a goose.

12

ON EASTER SUNDAY, SHORTLY BEFORE NOON, APRIL twenty-second of 1984, a breezy sunlit day with all of Catherine's numerous churches filled with flowers and soap-tightened faces, a part-time janitor at City Hall found the mayor's corpse upstairs in the courtroom.

The mayor sat slumped sideways in the witness box, freshly shaven, wearing a navy blue pinstripe suit, white shirt, and maroon knit necktie. As the janitor had told Boles on the phone, "He just sittin' there, Mister Orson, dressed fit to kill."

Mayor Leon Link gave the appearance of having dozed off in the witness chair, except for the smooth stone embedded in his temple near his silken, silvery sideburn. The rock, the size of a large red plum, was buried deep in the shell-thin bone. There was considerable blood on the cheekbone and jaw and it glistened also on the dark shoulder of the coat where it broke the pattern of the pinstriping.

When St. James arrived, Brenda Keeton and Boles and several plainclothes cops were on the scene, as was the mayor's son Rudell, a smug, muscular young man with a year-round tennis tan and a bucketful of snow-white teeth.

"I don't know what got into Daddy coming down here alone on the Sabbath," said Rudell, smiling incongruously, then straightening his lips and pulling a mournful face.

"What got into your daddy was a *rock*," Boles said, busy with the task of lifting prints.

"That's no way to talk," said Rudell, puffing up his cheeks and the muscles in his shoulders and chest.

"It's no worse than your standing around grinning like a jackass eating cuckleburrs," said Boles, not even bothering to look at the lawyer.

A rookie detective by name of Compton waved a piece of blue chalk and asked Boles how you marked the outline of the body when it was sitting in a chair. Boles, who was on one green polyester knee near the corpse, arose and said patiently: "Just mark around the chair, son, just make a little square there."

Brenda Keeton, who had phoned St. James at home, was absorbed with her note pad and pencil. After exchanging hellos they said nothing to each other or to anyone else for a while. Boles appeared to be going through the routine automatically, almost in a trance. Sweat rolled out of his crew cut down ruddy jowels into the collar of the lizard-green polyester shirt which today was illuminated by a necktie the color of Merthiolate. His lavender suspenders added to the overall glow of the good captain.

"Well, hoss," he said finally. "They say lightnin' don't strike twice in the same place, heh?"

"It didn't, Orson."

"I know, hoss, but awful close, wouldn't ya say?" He rubbed his eyes with the back of a wet, shaking hand.

"I don't know what to make of any of this. *Any* of it. Do you?"

St. James could only stand there staring at the body in the chair. Twice he opened his jaws, like a dog squaring off to bite at a flea, but no sound came out of him. Brenda was dead white and kept her eyes on the note pad. The coroner-ranger arrived and then the sheriff, bringing with him a couple of scared-looking deputies, all wearing sweaty Sherwood Forest green serge and modified western hats. They served with St. James and Brenda and several policemen as a coroner's jury. At the request of Boles, the verdict was left open pending further investigation.

The extent of Boles's shock was such that he did not abuse the coroner-ranger. When Nelson Barton snicked open the blade of his jackknife Boles simply held up a hand and said, "Naw, naw, we'll let the pathologist handle that this time."

St. James remembered the sickening sound of steel on bloody stone at the city dump the day Barton pried loose the stone. The rain splattering pink juice from the hole in the bone, the way it filled Barrington's ear. The rat popping out of the peach can, its tail naked and raw-looking in the rain.

The world was insane. Ten people gunned down in New York. Diplomats and government officials fair game all over the world. Death squads in El Salvador. The mess in Nicaragua. Hundreds of thousands, many of them children, dying in the Iran-Iraq holocaust. A woman gang-raped on a pool table in New Bedford, bystanders cheering the woman's attackers. In the overall view Little David was simply a natural progression of the general insanity. *Come to me and I will give thy flesh to the fowls of the air and the beasts of the field.* Killing was as old as the world. The Holy Bible ran red with blood. God drowned the whole damned Egyptian army. Even Moses was a murderer.

"I want to ask Orson some questions," Brenda whispered to St. James.

"Go ahead."

She looked apologetic. "It makes me self-conscious with you here."

"Why?"

"I don't know, it just does."

He patted her on the shoulder, trying not to look down at her bulging belly. He felt suddenly a surge of sympathy for this small, scared woman with the baby inside her, sorry for her and the whole lunatic planet. He left them and took the stairs down to the main floor and let himself out into the loveliness of the day. The people were headed home from church, cars filled with exhausted families wearing their painfully new Easter clothes, kids squalling and squealing, fathers grim with responsibility, mothers twisting around to slap at mutineers on the back seat. "Valerie, you do that one more time I'm going to slap the *tar* out a you." One child dumped a basketful of dyed eggs out of the window of a Chrysler station wagon. The car slowed, then kept going. The pink and blue eggs lay broken in the street, crinkled green paper grass scattering in the April wind.

The following day the town of Catherine was on show and the general populace loved it, the network television crews, newspaper and magazine reporters from a half-dozen of the nation's metropolitan centers.

The Barrington killing had made a mild news splash across the country; but the second terminal stoning really turned the trick. Whereas the initial incident was soon forgotten outside the southeastern sector, the carbon-copy homicide in which a stone and some unidentified weapon were used really stirred the top-salaried stratum of American journalism. The citizenry of Catherine was glued to television sets for the six o'clock newscasts. Sam Blather of CBS described the killing as "bizarre," posing the resounding question: "Is a madman loose in the confines of this sleepy, God-fearing town?" Krakow of NBC described the double slayings as "truly bizarre" and asked the world why, in a nuclear age, would anyone use such primitive weaponry. Pompostino of ABC, after a lengthy rigamarole which consisted almost verbatim of clipping from *The Catherine Call*, concluded that the situation was "shocking and bizarre." He asserted that residents of "this lazy, laid-back community will sleep tonight with one eye open—if, indeed, at all." All made a point of the fact Catherine lay in the heart of the Bible Belt. Blather said it was "ironic" that the slayings had distinct Biblical overtones.

Catherine residents looked eagerly in hopes of spotting someone they knew in film footage of City Hall and the rest of the dying downtown sector—Main Street between Sears and the Gulfway Railroad tracks. The Winston Rifles, a squad of elderly gentlemen who enjoyed dressing themselves in homemade Confederate uniforms, paraded for the visiting cameramen, firing a small brass cannon stuffed with paper towels and toilet paper. Twenty strong, they circled the Confederate statue on the County Courthouse lawn. The Hibbit Honeys also pranced and twirled for the network and the Shriners put on a show with their Krazy Kars and Turkish pantaloons. No one seemed to mind or even to care that neither of the dead city officials was a Shriner and that Hibbit Junior College was thirty miles south of Catherine. All this in the name of "local color," according to Blather, who also conducted man-on-the-street interviews. The question was: How do you feel about the cold-blooded murder of two members of your city council? A plumbing contractor stated, "I think it's a dang shame, makes the whole town look bad." An assistant librarian came up with, "I believe that when this business is solved and the culprit in custody we will find a very disturbed individual."

One man interviewed, an extremely wealthy architect named Crowell, said in his opinion the thing was "bizarre."

There was a twenty-one-inch black and white TV set high on a shelf at the Eagle Drugs and a similar set at Birdie's hamburger joint across the street on Main. Business doubled. Jane Pearley, glowing with motherhood and the loss of fifteen pounds, said on the *Today* program, which coincided with coffee and doughnuts at Birdie's and the Eagle Drugs, that Catherine, scene of the "bizarre" homicides, was "a very *spushel* kind of town, *espushelly* pretty this time of year."

Catherine, Alabama, was on the map.

Full-color shots of what was left of the azaleas, the glossy magnolias and pines, an arch of "stately" oaks in a residential area near St. James's home, a closeup of a plate of smoking hominy grits and eggs at Birdie's with the little Greek talking to the customer whom he had served. St. James knew from experience that Birdie probably had some of the grits on the thumb of his serving hand. Although the newspaperman was a native Southerner, he still considered grits an oddity. Perhaps even bizarre.

The local television station at WDOX was suddenly an instrument to be respected, particularly after the big names had departed with their costly camera equipment and forty-dollar haircuts. The news staff at WDOX, headed by a tubby little man who resembled a Pekinese with a shaved face, kept feeding the stuff to the network. There was Bellingham, the news chief, on national TV giving what he invariably described as *in-depth* reports of material which had been hashed and minced and rehashed. He did have one truly original piece which had not been lifted from the writings of St. James and Brenda Keeton—an exclusive interview with the head of Catherine's Water Department, Nathan Simmons, whose significance stemmed from the fact that he had worked with both the dead commissioner and the mayor and that the Water Department was located directly beneath the City Courtroom where the mayor met his untimely and "bizarre" end.

The Little David angle, which St. James had given to Brenda for one of her compact, no-nonsense pieces, was now national knowledge. "Where will Little David strike again?" Bellingham wanted to know and Blather and Krakow and Pompostino asked more than once in their deadpan, long-lipped newscasts from New York. People from Maine to California, from Sioux City to Pensacola, come to be as familiar with the Catherine city dump as they were with their own back yards.

Boles contended that St. James should have remained mum about Little David, that the publicity could drive him to cover and also made the scheduled slingshot competition appear rather obvious to anyone with half a brain. Boles decided to mask the intent of the contest by arranging a rich display of all kinds of weaponry and archery and handgun marksmanship events as well as the other.

"We'll have a nice prize in each division, hoss."

"Money?"

"I was thinking a beach towel for first and an umbrella for runner-up."

"That's pretty crummy, Orson."

81

"Waddaya mean?"

"Nobody's going to compete for that kind of junk—you might as well offer a pound of cough-drops."

"Maybe you're right, sport. Hell, I got an open mind."

"Fine."

"We talking menthol, or eucalyptus?"

13

FROM THE ROOF OF THE MOBLEY BANK BUILDING ST. James could see the green curve of the levee and the clay-laden red water beyond. A half-dozen cows the color of fudge grazed on the new grass. He bent forward to rest his weight on the parapet and the crumbling concrete stung his hands. The old iron bridge, no longer in use since the new one was built, glowed rustily in April sunlight and a cool breeze lifted dust from the top of the levee, the dust swirling pink against a pale blue sky.

He could hear Crystal behind him walking on the tarred gravel.

"Come look, Kiel." Crystal sounded excited. "Come look at this."

She was kneeling, the wind blowing her hair and when he went to her she showed him an area where someone had pried loose some of the stones. It had been done fairly recently; the tar was jet black, almost free of dust. "Whatta ya make of this?"

"I'm not sure," he said, her excitement contagious. "So some stones are missing."

83

"You know what I mean, don't try to be so darned cool, it's *tire*-some."

"All right, kid, if the impressions in the tar match the shape of the stones dug out of the skulls, this could be where the killer collected his ammo."

"Of course."

"So where does that leave us?"

"It's a start." Two days ago on assignment for a picture page of the wilting downtown sector of Catherine she'd taken an elevator to the tenth floor of the Mobley, then climbed the ladder to the roof. She had noticed the peculiar coloration of some of the rocks, but had not at first made the connection. The creamy quartz with narrow zigzag bands of bright brown and beige. She had taken photographs earlier of the rocks held in evidence by Boles.

"Okay, honey, we'll borrow the stones from Orson; or rather, we'll get him to come up here with us."

"Why does he have to come?"

"You know damned well he won't let the evidence out of his sight. He'll probably laugh his ass off about the whole thing."

Crystal arose and looked up at him. "If you were any more negative I could soak you in a tray of developer and make a picture from you."

He bent and kissed her lightly. Her lips were cushiony and tasted of Rolo and raspberry. Her ability to eat sweets incessantly and remain slim was one of the more mystifying items in her considerable bag of mysteries. The raspberry was her lipstick.

"Kissing's no answer." She lifted her chin and glowered.

"But it's awful nice, ain't it?"

"Sometimes."

* * *

Boles was anything but amused.

"I think the kid may have something there, hoss."

"She isn't a kid and I'm not a goddamned horse."

Boles scrabbled around in the upper lefthand drawer of his desk, fishing out a pair of brass knucks, a homemade knife and two dainty nickel-plated pistols. Then a jar of Vicks and an almost empty bottle of Scope and finally the rocks, swathed in tissue.

"C'mon, less go, if you waiting for me you backing up." Like much of Boles's rural route shit this made no sense, but it had a nice ring to it.

In less than fifteen minutes atop the Mobley Boles found what he was looking for, two impressions into which the curiously shaped stones appeared to fit almost exactly. There were minor discrepancies where the tar had pulled out along with the stones, but the detective said this was to be expected because they were stuck fast. A sergeant of police, who had brought along a kit that looked like a lunch bucket, importantly removed the powdered plaster and a bottle of water and stirred the mixture with a thumb, then made plaster casts of the two impressions under scrutiny. For some reason the water had what looked like broken bits of leaves in it and these gave his work an unusual appearance. A bristly, pastoral look.

"What's that stuff?" Boles said. "Where the hell you get that water, out the creek?"

"I'm sorry, chief."

"Sorry, my ass, next time put *clean* water in the bottle."

"Yessir."

"You can louse up the entire case with that kind of carelessness, sonny."

The sergeant stared down at the hardening casts and said, "I didn't fill the bottle this time, captain."

"Well, who the hell did?"

"You did, sir."

Boles spit tobacco juice into a Dixie Cup, then held it out to St. James who also spit into it. "You can't laugh with a mouthful a that shit," said the captain of detectives. "What's so funny, anyway?"

As they removed the lid of the trapdoor to descend the ladder Boles said, "I can't figger why, with all the rocks available, anybody would go up on a roof and pry rocks loose that are stuck in tar."

"Beats me," St. James said. "You're the ace detective."

"He may be back, a loony like that, you never know—I guess we'll have to stake it out."

"How do you hide men on a roof not much bigger than a tennis court, Orson?"

Boles grinned, punching the elevator button with a thick finger. "Why, hoss, we just roll 'em out flat and tar-an-gravel 'em."

"I'm serious, you can't set up any kind of a stakeout without concealment."

"We'll just have to do the best we can. The small housing for the stuff that operates the elevator and the two ventilators. Meantime I want some micrometer measurements on the rocks and the casts of the impressions. And thank Miss Crystal for me. We may solve this mess despite ourselves."

When they were back in Boles's unmarked police car St. James asked the detective if he'd turned up any kind of a line on Little David and Boles said no. He said he had no idea why the man was pestering a newsman instead of the police.

"I think it's more than pestering," St. James said. "I've a feeling he wants to plant one of those rocks in my head."

"Don't let him spook you, Kiel."

"It's not just me, the whole town's scared."

And that wasn't far from the truth. No doubt the three most apprehensive citizens at this point were the three members of the city council: the mayor's son, who was serving by appointment to fill his father's shoes until a special election could be held; Matthew Thames, a retired steamfitter who was inside commissioner, the only remaining member of the original council; and Sam Slade, interim commissioner in the post of C.B. Barrington. The residences of all three members of the council were under surveillance by police and a couple of cops were posted in the main corridor at City Hall during working hours. From the corridor the entrances of the councilmen's offices could be observed. Boles said that if he had his way every single unfamiliar person entering any of the offices would be checked out, searched, and questioned, but that this of course was not feasible, or even possible. Metal detectors were considered seriously but the idea was discarded because they would beep everything from ballpoint pens to pocket-change. Call-tracing equipment was connected with the telephone line at St. James's home. At least a score of possible suspects, including Goodbee and Dillard Harmon, had been interrogated at length by police, and the members of the department, along with sheriff's officers and those in the highway patrol, were alerted to be on lookout for "suspicious characters." Fingerprints and fibers collected at the scenes of the crimes thus far had proved of no value. Those from the roof of the Mobley had not even been sent off to the state crime laboratory, but Boles said this would be done promptly.

Boles said that although it was important to take all these measures when there were no witnesses to a crime, luck played an important role in the investigation. "We've worked together on a basketful of cases, hoss; and you know y'self the value of plain old blind-ass luck. Good example a that's Miss Crystal goin' up on that roof with her cameras to get them aerial shots a the downtown district. Suppose you didn't assign her to the story? And even after she was on the roof, who in hell's going to notice anything about the gravel up there? And if they did, how many would a been in a position to know what the killer's rocks look like?"

"He's still got a few of them in his shepherd's bag," said St. James.

"What's a shepherd's bag?"

"Search me."

No one knew better than St. James that for all his Good-Ole-Boy foolishness and posturing Orson Boles was a shrewd and relentless investigator. There had been several letters to the editor complaining that the detective had invaded privacy in his interrogation. Aside from routine questioning of people brought in by his assistants Boles had questioned a number of citizens who'd kicked up a rumpus about the size of ad valorem and personal property taxes—others who had raised Cain about water bills and tardy garbage collection. Still others with peeves about rezoning of property, increased traffic in residential neighborhoods, and even a few who had voiced rage when their pets were picked up by the city dogcatcher.

Boles's stamina was incredible. He could work night and day for months but seldom appeared exhausted, or even weary. The ketchup-and-cream complexion remained smooth as a schoolgirl's, the blue eyes clear as a baby's. His wife was bedridden with cancer of the pancreas and a mutual friend had told St. James that Boles nursed her through many a night of agony, she unable to sleep because of the pain.

As for his work on the current investigation, Boles

shrugged it off with a typical wisecrack: "Hoss, in a case like this it don't pay to leave a single stone unturned."

St. James declined to laugh.

"You get it, hoss? I mean the stone?"

"I get it."

"You just watch out you don't *really* get it—like right between the eyes."

"Orson, do you have Dillard Harmon and Goodbee under surveillance? I mean still?"

"Round the clock."

"And you've totally discounted the gunpowder traces on the stones?"

"I don't discount nothin', hoss. I'm hoping our weaponry show and competition will open some new avenues. Who knows?"

Who indeed?

If Little David was the killer and if he was dumb enough to keep making phone calls, maybe, just maybe, he was stupid enough to show up next week with his sling, or blunderbuss, or whatever.

Like Boles said, a great deal depended on blind-ass luck.

But apparently no luck was involved in the marksmanship of the killer. In each instance the stone was lodged where it would cause maximum damage. The stone in the mayor's head was the only one found in the courtroom, where it would have been fairly simple to locate a rock that had missed its target. Such a survey for misfired missiles was of course close to impossible at the city dump. Whoever brought off the murders would have had small chance for a second shot. Boles said it was reasonable to assume that the victims knew the killer and had no idea what he was up to until it was too late. "You make a heap a enemies in politics, Kiel," said Boles. "Not only the man you beat and what you may have said about him in whipping his ass—but every member of his family and all his friends don't feel too friendly toward you. The one that comes to my mind is Johnny Trask. He ran a shit-slinging race against Barrington for the outside commissioner post. And C.B. slung it right back at him."

St. James sought to dredge up the name and the man, John Trask. And then he remembered that Crystal said Trask was a lifelong buddy of Stephanie's husband, the taciturn truck doctor at the city barn.

14

JOHN TRASK WAS IN AN ACUTE STAGE OF HANGOVER. SOME-
one in the back of the building was revving a bike engine
and each time it screamed Trask squinched his eyes shut.
Finally he picked up the phone and called the back-shop
and said, "Jim, who the hell's trying to tear the guts out
a that bike?" A pause, eyes still closed, lids quivering,
"Well, tell him to *quit* it."

Trask opened his eyes. They looked like wet licorice
drops. "The old lady and me were up all night. I aint
what I used to be with the boudoir acrobatics."

"You look fine," said St. James, impatient to get on
with the interview.

"I use to do it all night," said Trask. "Now it takes
me all night to do it."

Beyond the door of Trask's office St. James could see
the gleaming ranks of new motorcycles. Massive four-
cylindered Aspencades with all the extras, windshields
affixed to streamlined farings, radio, plastic trunks, more
pipes than a church organ. An assortment of Interstates
and Silverwings, glittering scarlet and black. Some 750's

and 400's and a sassy-looking black Ascot 500, very lean and functional among the fatter bikes.

"Pretty, aint they?" said Trask, who had made a small fortune selling motorbikes, but never rode one himself. "I'd like to put you on one a them Ascots." In past years he had sold St. James a dozen bikes. Almost every spring and sometimes in the fall when the weather was crisp and golden St. James would get the bike fever. If the price was right he could ride it six months or maybe a year and get most of his money out of it.

"I didn't come here to buy a bike, John." But he had difficulty tearing his eyes loose from the damned things, particularly the Ascot.

"I know, but that *is* your kind of a bike, no garbage bolted onto it, plenty of engine but not too much. That bike'll top out around a hundred and ten miles an hour. "I wouldn't be ascared to head for California on that little sucker."

"You don't ride bikes."

Trask tried to smile, but apparently it hurt his head. He closed his eyes again and said, "I mean if I did."

"We have reason to believe there was bad blood between Dillard Harmon and C.B. Barrington. Can you tell me anything about that?"

"I can tell you that Barrington was a bed-hopping little cockroach who got what was coming to him."

"Did Barrington have something going with Stephanie?"

Trask took his time answering. He shucked a couple of Alka-Seltzers out of the foil and plopped them into a glass of water. "I don't know for sure, but Dillard thought so. He use to knock off work in the middle of the day and drive by their house looking for the bastard's car."

"But he never caught them together?"

"Not as far as I know. Dillard can be pretty tight-mouthed about some things. I think he thinks just about everybody is balling the redhead."

"Are they?"

"I don't know."

"Did you ever?"

Trask tried to look indignant. "What kinda question's that, Kiel? Dillard's my pal."

"Okay, did you ever hear Dillard say anything to the effect he was angry enough to do harm to Barrington? Really hurt him?"

"What you asking me is do I think Dillard killed the sonofabitch. Do I know anything that would help the police sink their claws in my friend. The answer is no, and even if I did I wouldn't tell. Any dumbass would know that. Hell, I had more reason than Dillard to fix that cocksucker's wagon—and I wasn't even in town the day it happened. I was in Baton Rouge picking up a load a three-wheelers."

"Can you verify that?"

"Of course."

"You may just have to do that, John."

"Fine with me." Trask staged a phony yawn, arising from the desk, stretching, arching his back and covering his mouth with a hand. "Now come out here and lemme show you that bike."

"I don't want a bike," St. James said without conviction. The old feeling began stealing into him, the bike-hunger. "I really don't, John. I'm getting too old for that kind of thing. If I laid it down in the road they'd never finish picking up the pieces of these brittle old bones."

"Bull."

"No, I mean it." They were standing now in the main

showroom. Glitter and glow of enamel and engine-fins, smell of new rubber. The Ascot looked as if it were going ninety miles an hour even when it was standing still.

"Bull, look here at the way the filler cap on the gas tank locks. Air-shocks up front, disc brakes front and back. Take you a hundred miles on a sniff a gas, boy."

"I've got a ten-speed bicycle, hundred miles on a Coca-Cola. I don't *need* a motorcycle and I don't *want* one."

"All right, Kiel, you the doctor." Trask shrugged and rubbed his temples, using fingertips of both hands. Of Syrian descent and as canny as a Middle-Eastern rug merchant, he knew exactly when to back off the hard sell. "Why you holding your mouth all pipped up like that? You look like a bass that swallowed a bad bug."

"Got to spit, widdaminit." St. James went out the front door and spit on the asphalt parking space. He was dying for a cigarette. The chewing tobacco ordinarily gave some relief, but today it only seemed to sharpen his need for a Kool Filter King. He imagined breathing deeply of the mentholated smoke. When he turned to reenter the door he saw the black Ascot. Trask was wiping it gently with a red flannel rag, stroking it, fondling it. It seemed to arch its gas-tank against Trask's soft, slow-moving rag. Trask was wearing one of those white, pleated, tails-out Cuban shirts. It was made of very thin, almost-sheer cotton and you could see the green of a pack of Kools in the breast pocket.

"Anything wrong?" he asked St. James when he rejoined him in the showroom.

"No."

"How much were you spending on cigarettes when you quit?" Trask said.

"About three dollars a day."

"That's ninety a month, right?"

"I guess so."

"You could take this bike home with you for a couple hundred down and ninety a month."

Back at Trask's desk the motorcycle magnate began scribbling figures on a pad, monthly interest on the loan, state sales tax, cost for securing title. St. James had the familiar stunned, sick feeling he always had when he was on the verge of buying something expensive, a sort of muffled helplessness. Trying to regain composure, he asked Trask if he planned to run again for the job of outside commissioner. Still scribbling, Trask said he wasn't certain, but that they ought to get someone in there to try to revitalize the downtown section. "It's a crying shame," he said. "Did you ever get up on the Mobley and look down at that dead street?"

"Yes, I have."

"You can see the whole town from up there."

St. James said nothing and Trask went into a long rigamarole about how only a few years ago Main Street was the heart of the business district. "The town's dying in the middle and kind of melting out to the edges." He said that a forward-looking city administration could change all that. "Lack of parking space is what killed it. We need some multi-story parking facilities, the kind you see in Birmingham and New Orleans. Catherine's growing, man, we got more than forty thousand people counting the college enrollment. Did you know that?"

Trying to keep the excitement out of his voice St. James asked," How'd you happen to go up on top the Mobley?"

"Lookit here, Kiel, your payments would come to ninety-nine dollars and ninety-nine cents a month with this special promotional price on the Ascot. It's a steal if there ever was one. It's an eighty-four model but brand new and at eleven hundred you're getting that beauty for half price. What the hell, you only go around once."

"Let me think about it, John." He considered the good and bad aspects of pressing Trask on the question about the climb to the top of the bank and decided it would not be an intelligent thing to do at this point. God knows he'd done enough bumbling in previous investigations in the case. Could Trask be Little David? Had he had that much venom in him for the man who humiliated him at the polls? And what about the mayor's death? Did Trask hate him, too?

"Take all the time you want," said Trask. "I'm not goin' anywhere."

St. James could contain it no longer: "What were you doing up on the bank, John? That's a pretty rickety ladder to the trapdoor, heh?"

"I been up there a lot. Mostly I just like to look out at the river and there's always a breeze, even in August. You know? I started going up there when I was a little kid. My step-dad was a dentist. Had an office on the tenth floor. I remember he'd give me little sample jars of Horlick's powdered malted milk and I'd go up top and look out at the river and stick the tip a my tongue in the jar. No other taste in the world like that. There was a picture of a blue cow on the jar. It would get gummy and I always wanted to throw it off the roof to the street, but I never did. I wanted to be a Scout and I knew it wasn't the thing for a Scout to do."

"I fired a slingshot off the roof," St. James lied, watching Trask's face for reaction.

But there was none. "You could a hurt somebody. How long ago was that?"

"Oh, I don't know, a long time," still watching Trask for reaction. "I was pretty handy with a sling when I was a kid."

"Yeah, me too—but I never had the guts to . . . oh, well, how 'bout the bike, you finished thinking?"

"Okay, John, it's a deal."

"We'll have to service it out and put a charge on the battery. I guarantee you won't regret buying it."

"I already do."

They shook hands on it and St. James returned to the newspaper. He was both sick and happy about the bike. As for the results of the interrogation, he'd made at least a bit of progress. One more chip to try and fit into the puzzling mosaic. He felt that if he did not smoke a cigarette within the hour he would flip his lid as high as the roof of the Mobley. The corners of his mouth burned from an excess of Red Man.

That afternoon when the paper was put to bed Crystal drove him to the Honda place and he picked up the bike, which had been waxed, polished, and oiled up and the seat had been glossed with Armor-All protectant. It was a lovely thing, balanced and bright and it roared to life at the touch of the electric starter.

He met Crystal at his house and he went inside and dug around in his closet until he found the two old visored helmets, one silver and one white. He'd bought the white one for May but after a couple of rides she'd had it with bikes.

Crystal left the Jag in the front yard and climbed up behind him on the Ascot FT 500, setting her booted feet firmly on the footpegs like an old-timer. "Come on boss, kick her in the tail and let's go," she said. Her breasts were burning holes in his back and she had her arms tight around him. The girl across the street waved her hose at them. She had planted three clumps of ligustrum near the street and was watering them and the snarly yellow dog also was watering one of them. "You quit that, Rocky," the girl shouted. "You quit that this minute, you hear." When the bike started, Rocky ran slantingly into the brick street eyeing St. James's leg speculatively. St. James kicked out at him but missed and the bike wobbled on down to the intersection and hung a right beneath the arched oaks. The cream-colored palace of the deceased mayor was on the corner and the widow, in cream-colored shorts, was washing a cream-colored Cadillac. She waved her squirting hose at them. It seemed to St. James that the waving hoses were symbolism at its worst. One of Crystal's hands slid down to his belly.

On the Interstate he twisted the throttle hard and the bike jumped forward as the tachometer needle hopped to seven thousand RPM's. The speedometer dial said they were doing about eighty miles an hour by the time they had travelled a half mile. There seemed to be nothing coming from behind, although the rear-vision mirrors were vibrating so that you could not really see anything in them. They swooped past an exit with a sign that read: FOOD, GAS, LODGING. And another that said: REST STOP, NO RESTROOMS.

Thirty miles or so from Catherine he eased off on the throttle, afraid he would damage the engine if he did not allow oil to come up around the cylinders at full flow and bathe the new parts. In time the moving parts would hone themselves. He dropped it down to sixty and ahead of him, far down the road, he saw a sixteen-wheeler easing into the road, looking big as a boxcar. The tractor-trailer rig took neither the left nor the right lane but rode the middle stripe, the driver apparently oblivious of the motorbike, or not caring.

Finally the big rig pulled lazily over to the right-hand lane. St. James could hear the whuffing of its overhead exhaust, a deep sound in the lighter sounds of the bike and the buffeting of the wind. As he swung out to pass he felt, rather than heard, the car on his left and then he was caught between the two. He was looking almost directly into the meat-eating wheels on his right, they looking now as large as the wheels on earth-moving equipment; and when he tried to gun out of the squeeze both the car and truck accelerated, or so it seemed to him. The noise was unbelievable and the relatively light-weight bike could not be held steady in the slipstreams. He thumbed the horn on the bike and it sounded like a baby bleating in a wind tunnel.

The automobile began edging in on him, forcing him by degrees toward the wheels of the truck. All three vehicles were nailed at seventy-five miles an hour and whenever he tried to gun the bike out of the slot the car angled shallowly to hold him. It was a Datsun 280-Z which looked to have been painted with red lead. The windows were dark, almost black, so that he could see roughly the shape of a figure at the wheel, but no colors or details.

Crystal's nails dug into his chest but he barely felt them and she had her head pressed close to him so that their hard helmets chattered. At one point his right rear-view mirror touched the silver skin of the trailer and the car to his left was no more than an arm's length distant. *What a way to go*, he thought. *Brand new bike. Prettiest day of the year. Prettiest girl. Prime of one's middle-age.*

He veered left bumping the car hard with his leg and the front wheel of the Honda skittered, his footpeg snagging against the side of the Datsun. Shriek of rubber, howling hiss of wind, and as if in slow motion, the action masked by the uniform speed of the three vehicles, he saw suddenly the startled face of the trucker in the rig's California mirror, the rounded eyes and mouth, the crimped bill of a blue baseball cap. Air brakes squealed and as the rig pulled off onto the shoulder smoking rubber the Datsun took off.

Crystal yelled, "Let's try to catch him."

"I don't want him."

"That thing was trying to murder us, Kiel."

"I know." His knees were shaking so badly he felt he could not support the weight of the bike after they pulled onto the shoulder. They were not shaking the way knees shake when you are cold or exhausted. They were going knock-knock-knock like in the funny papers. They were bumping the bike so hard it hurt.

"Did you get his tag number, Kiel?"

"No."

"Me either." She was stroking his belly, still sitting behind him on the stepped-up passenger portion of the seat.

The truck driver, who was out of Tuscaloosa with a load of asphalt shingles and bathroom mirrors, told them he had not laid eyes on the bike until the moment before he veered off the road to give them room. "I'm sorry, mister, I'm 'bout half blind with hemorrhoids. Too much time on the road. Can't shit regular, begging your pardon ma'am."

"That's all right," said Crystal. "My grandmother used to put pine needles in a slop-jar and pour boiling water over them and then sit down and steam herself, have you tried that?"

"Well, no ma'am, I never did."

"You try it." There was genuine sympathy in her voice. Here was another wounded animal which needed her attention. "Grandma Bunt said pine-steam did the trick, that compared to it, Preparation-H was no better than peanut butter."

"I'll give her a try." He seemed to be peering at a stand of pines atop a grassy slope to the right. "I be damn, *pine*-steam."

"My grandmother said the people way back in covered wagons carried pine-tops wrapped in wet blankets wherever they went."

"I don't reckon cactus-steam would a worked," said the driver, offering St. James a chew from a brand new pouch of Red Man. When St. James dug into it and filled his cheek, the driver looked pleased, as if a bond had been established there in the diesel stink on the shoulder of the road. "Nice bike you got there. New, aint she?"

"Yes," said St. James. "Did you get the car's license number?"

"He didn't have none, there wasn't nothing in the bracket. I got to be shoving on down the road. You folks be careful."

"You can depend on it," said St. James, his knees almost steady now, only a mild shivering in them. He clopped his clear plastic visor down over his face and said to Crystal, "You ready?"

"Yes, let's go home." Then to the trucker who was ploding back to his rig, "You try those pine-tops, you hear?"

The bike was overheated and would not start immediately. St. James was still trying to crank it when the diesel rig lumbered past. There was a picture of a running camel painted on the silver side of the trailer. And the words: WE'RE HUMPING TO PLEASE.

In a minute or so the Ascot came to life. After a time they reached a cloverleaf exit and swung right, then hung a left and rode over the interstate on a new concrete bridge, getting back on the northbound lanes to Catherine. St. James's head was busy recording incidents of

101

the past half hour and his cheeks were ballooned with tobacco juice. He spit a squirt and it simply hung in the air in front of him. This seemed odd. When you spit it was supposed to go away, not hang there. It occurred then to him that he had forgotten to raise his face mask before spitting. He had to stop and wipe out the inside of the mask, Crystal yowling helplessly. The juice had dripped onto the chest of his best plaid shirt and some of it was in his lap. "Shut up," he said; and then he, too, began laughing. They got off the bike and she used a bandanna to help clean him. She was suddenly serious. "That man in the Datsun really meant to finish you, Kiel."

"What about you?"

"Me too, but I think he was after you—I think that was your Little David."

"Could be, or it could've been some drunk trying to scare us."

"I don't think so."

"Could you see him through the windows, kid?"

"No, except he seemed to be tall. It looked like his head was rubbing the top of that little car."

"Well, Boles can round up all tall men driving 280-Zs heh?"

"I love you," she said. "I don't know what I'd do if anything happened to you."

"You'd probably have to go to work."

A mile or so outside the city limits of Catherine St. James saw something red in his mirror. He reached out and tried to steady the vibrating glass but could not make out the shape of the car which was expanding steadily in the mirror.

The bike was creeping along now and Crystal twisted around to look and as she did a blood-red Porsche swerved from behind them in the slow lane, a young girl, probably of junior-high-school age, was standing on her knees beside the driver waving back at them and smiling, coppery curls blowing in the wind.

"You're trembling," Crystal said in his ear, their helmets knocking together.

"Tell me about it."

"We'll be fine when we get home," she said. He could hear her clearly when the bike was not speeding and again he was becoming conscious of the breasts against his back.

"They probably thought I was your father," he said, not without bitterness.

15

Jack Elwood, general manager of *The Catherine Call*, resplendent in his amber shooting glasses, navy blazer, and slacks of exactly the proper corporate shade of gray, loved to preside over the regular weekly meeting of the news staff. This despite the fact he had majored in aeronautical engineering and could not write a news lead or even a decent letter or interoffice memo. Inmates of the business office admitted grudgingly that Elwood had "a fine head for figures" but he had about as much business in a news-staff conference as a cockroach in a bathtub—and was approximately as conspicuous. He was not simply ignorant of the many problems of collecting and writing the news. He was oblivious to them.

When St. James and the others were seated, Elwood sat, back straight, chin high and steady, the fluorescent light bouncing off the gold-rimmed glasses. "Good afternoon, team," he intoned.

No one said anything.

"Mr. St. James," said Elwood, "it has been called to

my attention that you are spending less and less time in the newsroom. Have you anything to say to that?"

"I get the job done, Jack."

"In your opinion."

"Yes."

"Mr. St. James, you hired on here as a city editor, not as an assistant to Mr. Orson Boles, is that correct?"

"No."

"How is that, sir?" Lifting of lemon-colored eyebrows.

"When I hired on I was a reporter. That was quite a while ago. You weren't here."

Elwood cleared his throat and sat motionless and silent. This was one of his favorite acts. The Big Menace. Man with the Ax. "I didn't come in here to bicker with you, St. James. I want to know why you find it necessary to spend so much time outside the building."

"I consider the murder of two members of the city council worth digging into, don't you?"

"Never mind that."

"It's top priority on our news list," said St. James. "If we can have a hand in breaking it, we will have a leg up on the TV people—access to background they can't possibly have."

"I thought Miss Brenda Keeton was your police reporter," said Elwood, smiling now and looking around the table to see if he had scored. Not a peep out of anyone. Faces still. "Correct me if I'm wrong, Mr. St. James."

Brenda opened her mouth to speak, then changed her mind. Her lips were very puffed and bitten today and her belly swelled against the edge of the long, polished walnut conference table. Some days she looked as if her husband had tried to eat her lips off.

St. James, looking now at Brenda beside him, placed a hand on her hand on the table and said, "Brenda is doing a splendid job on the running day-to-day story, often with very thin material to work with. I feed her a few additional items when I can do it without hampering the investigation."

"You make Miss Keeton sound like a trained seal. I understand she is quite competent to gather information on her own."

St. James sat back in the slippery chair, toying with a crystal paperweight. It was a glass ball with little blue fishes in it and when you shook the ball it agitated them and they darted everywhichaway. The editor looked up from the ball finally and into the blank amber shooting glasses. He appeared to be pondering what Elwood had said; but actually he was thinking what an exquisite relief it would be to bounce the ball off the sleek blond head, perhaps shattering the ball so that all the little blue fishes swam in the perfumed oil on the head of the general manager.

"Would you repeat that, sir?" St. James said, dragging out the words and turning loose of the temptation of the paperweight. "Not that about the trained seal, I mean the other stuff."

"What other stuff?" Elwood clearly was losing both his corporate cool and most of his menace and there was a titter around the table as St. James said, "Gosh, Jack, I don't see how you expect us to remember what you say when you don't know yourself."

Open laughter now from Brenda and Linda Comstock, the little lady who wrote reviews of books and plays and music recitals out at the college. Constance, the society editor sat frozen in her chair as did Conroy the Britishy Sunday editor from Minnesota. You could hear the cricking of the stem of his Comoy pipe as he clamped down on it in an effort to look austere. Barney the sports editor was dozing and would not awaken until his name was called for weekly scheduling of coverage of local events. Barney's Eskimo eyes were half open, but he was faraway, browsing in that mysterious pasture of the mind where sports editors go during conversation unrelated to sex or moist muscle. Kenny, the executive editor, was on vacation in Florida, which was best, because he detested scenes. Myrick, the assistant city editor, was having an impacted molar chiseled out of his hairy jaw.

Elwood, realizing now that he was losing control, turned on Brenda. "Do you find this amusing, Miss Keeton?"

"No sir, no indeed."

"Mrs. Comstock?"

"Landsake no," said Linda Comstock, her stiff, hennaed hair shaking. "I guess I'm just nervous, Mr. Elwood."

"As for you, St. James, you've not heard the last of this. Let me see you in my office when the meeting is adjourned."

"Yessir," said St. James. He walked a tender edge with the general manager. Any abrupt gust of emotion in the general manager could prove terminal. The sonofabitch could fire you, and without Kenny here as an intermediary, Elwood was patently dangerous. Everyone had been walking on eggs since Elwood took over the operation following the death of John Robinson. Elwood never seemed to be able to make up his mind whether to be a Regular Fellow or a hardnosed SNA executive. Sometimes he went around slapping backs and saying, "Great team play on that flood story," and laughing his Mortimer Snerd laugh. And within the hour he was a steel-spined prick who seemed to be mad at the world. Crystal said it was insecurity, that he had bitten off more responsibility than he could gracefully chew. Maybe so, but in any case it was a resounding pain in the ass.

Sometimes the city editor almost missed John Robin-

107

son. Robinson was at least predictable. You knew that on Friday he would be just as mean as he was on Monday. He never slapped backs or tried to fraternize with the troops.

Briscoe Risk, who was on daily assignment at Pimm and not required to attend the weekly review and planning conferences, limped into the newsroom, his khakis dusted with salt. They were tunneling in solid salt at Pimm, still testing the site as a possible nuclear-waste disposal facility. "Hello everybody," Risk said, waving his note pad.

When no one spoke he looked up at St. James and said, "Hey, who died?"

"We're not sure yet," said St. James. "How're things in the Big Hole?"

"You can't pin them down. They've cut fifty miles of tunnel in that salt and they still say it's only an experiment, that we won't know for months if we get the nuclear garbage."

"You had enough of it? Joe would love the assignment."

"Heck no, the only thing I had before this was the building of the sewage-treatment lagoon. Salt beats doodoo, any way you slice it." Briscoe, who had been a correspondent for IWS during World War II, was a lanky ruin of a man who had been St. James's bureau chief during the New Orleans days; but the bottle had laid him low and when he'd hit St. James for a job a year before he was a sick man. He'd lost his old friends and his family and he came to Catherine in a broken-down Hudson Hornet with little else besides the clothes on his back. He had chronic osteomylitis in his right leg and the miracle drugs apparently had arrested infection, but could not cure it. "Why all the long faces?" Risk asked St. James now.

St. James told him.

"I don't understand the man," said Risk. "He's either slobbering on you or trying to stomp you. You want me to try to talk to him?"

"It wouldn't help."

"I don't know, I've become his pet for some reason. He had me out to his house to meet his wife and little kids. I didn't know what to say. He kept one of his little girls in his lap the whole time and he would kiss her cheek over and over until it was red. It made the hell of a smacking noise. His wife held the other child in her lap and we rocked and rocked on the front porch. The wife looked delighted at all of Jack's kissing. She giggled and looked at me and said, 'When Daddy finds a sweet spot he stays on it.'"

"You've got to be making that up," said St. James, who had never witnessed Elwood in the family setting.

"Let me talk to him," Briscoe said, grinning his exhausted Joel McCrea smile. "Maybe I can find Daddy's sweet spot."

"Suppose you don't?"

"I been fired before, remember?" Briscoe arose and limped jauntily around the Great Barrier Reef, a varnished plywood partition separating the newsroom from classified and display advertising. As creaky and old as he was, and he had to be in his sixties, he had the guts of a burglar.

In a little while he returned and said, "Jack says to tell you he was in a foul mood and had no right to take it out on you and the others."

"What'd you say to him?"

"I said that you were training Myrick so he could take over the city desk on your vacation in May. I pulled an SNA memo off the bulletin board, the one emphasizing the importance of cross-training. Jack said he hadn't even read it. And I said that you saw Mrs. Elwood and the kids at The Eagle Drugstore and thought they were about the cutest things you ever laid eyes on."

"Good Lord," said St. James, letting out his breath. "Are the kids really cute?"

"Do you think hamsters are cute?"

"Sort of."

"Well, both kids look like hamsters."

St. James threw most of the afternoon mail into the wastebasket as usual. No matter how many envelopes you ripped open there seemed always to be more, an unrelenting cascade of junk on family reunions, hair-dresser conventions, pending rock concerts by unheard-of groups with names like Hard Howl or Distant Cry or the Packard Clippers. He could not believe that Briscoe Risk had simply sailed into Elwood's walnut-paneled lair and gotten him off the hook. Nor could he imagine Elwood dandling a baby. Slobbering on the Sweet Spot.

St. James had to admit to himself that Elwood was on solid ground in his latest tirade. The city editor recognized the fact that he was neglecting his newspaper job and had been for weeks, ever since the investigations began. He and Boles had worked together over the years on a dozen cases and were remarkably successful as a team. Now law officers throughout the area and in adjacent states were trying to locate a red Datsun sports car with dark windows. Gangster windows. There were at least two red 280-Z's in Catherine, both belonging to doctors.

Boles questioned both of them in the presence of Crystal and St. James. The captain of detectives said that although the windows of their cars were clear, not smoky, the local Auto-Shak Co. sold a dark-gray, almost black, film which could be cut to fit any automobile window.

The doctors questioned separately were pompous and

terrified, a comical combination. One of them had repaired a hernia for Boles and sought to establish an air of rapport by calling him Orson. It was ineffectual. Yet in the light of their answers, to Boles it was reasonably clear that neither had sought to jam the motorcycle under the wheels of the tractor-trailer. One of the two cars was not even the right shade of red, a hue which would remain burned into the newsman's memory for life. An orange-red, the color of Swift's Meatpacking vehicles, very little gloss. You saw it on old-timey steel bridges as a first coating preparatory to painting, on certain ironwork during construction.

St. James thought, but was not certain, that he had seen a long gouge on the front quarter-panel, a deep, painted-over blemish in the skin of the car. Crystal would neither confirm nor deny this. She said it was possible, but that she was too frightened to see much of anything.

Neither of the doctors' cars was gouged. Both were immaculate inside and out, having been washed and vacuumed at The Red Arrow across the street from the clinic where they worked. Boles appeared interested in this, also in whether the footpeg of the bike had made any kind of a mark when it thumped the door of the car. No mark.

Boles later asked St. James why he hadn't at least tried to hang onto the tail of the Datsun long enough to get a tag number. "Hoss, you blew it, I guess you know that."

"I told you what the truck driver said—there wasn't a tag."

"Why didn't you chase him anyway? Miss Crystal says that silly bike a yours will bump up around a hundred."

"I didn't want to burn it up."

"Miss Crystal says you were running ninety with her on the back end."

Crystal looked embarrassed, a slow flush spreading

111

upward from cheeks to cheekbones. "I'm sorry, Kiel, I wasn't trying to make trouble or put you in a bad light, you ought to know that."

St. James said, "Honey, would you go out in the hall and let me talk to this dumb sonofabitch a minute?"

When she was gone he said to Boles, "Orson, there's no way a new bike can catch a Datsun 280-Z. On top of that, if you did manage it he could knock you off the road or poke a pistol out the window and blow your head off."

"Sure," said Boles.

"All right," said St. James. "So I was scared shitless."

"Now we're getting somewhere, hoss."

"And also I didn't want to get Crystal hurt."

"Sure, hoss, the old chivalry, what?" Boles spit into his perpetual Dixie Cup, very daintily. He could make it look as if he were sipping a Coke or something from the cup. He held out the cup to St. James who loosed a rich squirt of Red Man into it. Just one cigarette, if only he could light up a cigarette and drag smoke down to his balls and never smoke another one. But it didn't work that way. If he smoked one he would burn three packs of the goddamned things before he went to bed tonight. Oscar Wilde had it right. The little cylinders gave pleasure, but never satisfaction. You commenced wanting another before you were finished with the one in your mouth.

"And maybe," said Boles, "he wouldn't a smeared you all over the concrete or blown your head off. I'm not faulting you for being scared. The whole town's scared. You don't see much health-walking or jogging these days. I done quit jogging myself."

"I noticed. I'm grateful."

"Like I was saying, maybe he wouldn't a tried to do you in if you caught him. Maybe he would a just got out of that little Japanese car and whipped your ass in front of Miss Crystal, heh?"

112

"You think of everything, Orson, don't you?"

"Where's your bike parked now?"

"On the lot at the newspaper."

"I want to try scraping for a paint sample on the foot-peg."

"The peg's made of rubber-covered metal and there isn't anything on it."

"Okay, but if you see one a my men kneeling beside the bike, don't get your ass in a uproar."

"Okay, I'll be brave."

Boles smiled and spit, running the flat of his hand lightly across the top of the auburn bristles on his head. "It's about time, ain't it hoss?"

Scattered around Boles's rectangular office, which also served as home base for three other detectives and three members of the department's Narc squad, were various weapons he intended to display at the show Sunday in Compton State Park west of town. There were bows and crossbows borrowed from a local sporting-goods store for the day to be used in the competition. On a filing cabinet littered with assorted remnants of evidence used in past trials were the two slingshots Boles had made, neither of which St. James and Boles had gotten around to testing properly. Boles said he had tried them with ball bearings for ammo and that he could not hit the inside wall of a barn if he were locked inside it. Atop the same bank of cabinets St. James saw a homemade knife which had brass knucks welded to it for a handle, a curved throwing stick that looked like a very narrow jai-alai basket, four rusted machetes, a Smith & Wesson .357 Magnum that had been nickel-plated and fitted with a special trigger modification, three old .22 Remington pumps from Boles's personal collection, a 20-gauge sawed-off shotgun which had cost the life of a young patrolman answering a call to a bank heist, four rubber-powered slingshots also on loan from Dee's Sporting Goods, these almost identical to the one St. James had found in the shanty of Robert Goodbee. On the floor fronting the long line of filing cabinets against the wall were empty soft drink, beer, and whiskey bottles to be used as targets. Some of the bottles had not been completely emptied and the stink of stale beer and bourbon was strong in the room.

Boles said he had shortened the name of the competition to The Weaponry Show. This St. James already knew, but he said nothing. Boles had run four ads in *The Catherine Call*, each two columns wide by six inches deep.

"Orson, any fool would know what you're up to," said St. James. "I mean, really, do you expect the killer to come busting into the park to knock a bottle to pieces with one of those things?"

"Could be. Dumber things have happened."

"It just doesn't make much sense," said St. James. "I don't think you're going about this the right way."

"What's the right way, hoss?"

"I don't know."

"Me neither, but I'm going to do *something*—even if I do it wrong. We can't just sit around with our thumbs up our ass waiting for him to knock you off or wipe out the entire city council. Have you been to a council meeting since the killings?"

"No."

"They don't even look at each other, they all staring at the door. When Hattie comes in with the coffee tray they sit stiff as ramrods in their seat, rolling their eyes and looking like they about to piss all over theirself."

"You can't blame 'em."

"When they aren't up there being scared they over here at my place. How come I haven't caught the killer?

Shouldn't I at least have some decent leads? What the hell am I doing about all this? And the mayor's son is the worst of the lot. You would think he's a real mayor with all his airs. I jailed him one night when he was in high school, caught him and his date stiff-starch nekkid in the back of a camper in city park. I shone a flashlight inside and he started pulling it out of her, I swear a yard of cock. I thought the pissant never would get it all out."

"I don't see how you can hold that against him, Orson."

"If you ever saw the length a my little stub, hoss, I believe you'd understand."

"I can wait."

"He was a cold-eyed little motherfucker when he was a kid. When his Daddy came down to the station to bail him out he treated the old man like dirt. Wouldn't barely talk to him. I never have forgotten that, the rotten little bastard just stared at the old man, like he was ashamed of him, instead of it being the other way around. The kid was always in trouble. Mostly minor stuff, but a lot of it, stealing gearshift knobs off used car lots, trying to crowbar a bronze plate off Dickey Hall, the girls' dormitory at the college, shooting out streetlights with an air-rifle. And then he went to Ole Miss and to law school there and when he came home you'd a thought he was Mister Priss. He'd got hisself born again along with the law degree. Sometimes he teaches a Young People's Sunday School class. He helped raise money to rebuild the pet shelter across the tracks, handled the turkey-baskets for the Optimists Christmastime. He makes me want to puke; and he knows it. You heard him mushmouthing up in the courtroom when we found his dad's body. 'I don't know what got into Daddy coming down here on the *Sabbath*.' "

"Is he sincere?"

115

"Hell, hoss, I don't know who's *sincere*. I don't even know if I'm sincere. But whatever I am, I ain't a cobra dressed up like a garden hose."

"No, you dress like a lizard."

"I just like green. I happen to really like it."

"A green polyester lizard," said St. James, his vanity still wounded by Boles's questions about the aftermath of the trouble with the Datsun and the sixteen-wheeler.

16

COMPTON STATE PARK WAS A SERENE AND DAZZLING PLACE in early spring before the tourists began pouring in to soak up The Southern Experience, asking wide-eyed questions about the vestigial remains of the Confederacy. Some of them wanted to know if Southerners really talked that way all the time and others appeared disappointed to discover there was really no great deal of difference between North and South once you got past "that cute accent." You got the impression they expected everyone in Alabama to be living on plantations, in manor houses with silver doorknobs still taking a blacksnake whip to sassy blacks whenever it could be done without getting caught. There were a few visitors this time of year in campers or in the tidy brick cottages along the edge of Lake Compton, which was dug by National Guard engineers during the second world war, with considerable help from German POW's. In the beginning it was Thompson State Park and Thompson Lake and then Biggerstaff Park & Lake, and only two years past had

117

Governor Lance Compton changed it. Every time the state elected a new governor one of the first things he did was to commence naming lakes and parks after himself. No matter, it was a beautiful part of the world with its pine-studded slopes and the expanse of ice-cold water from seven ice-cold creeks, complete with enough firm-fleshed fish to delight the heart of any serious fishermen and enough water mocassins to allow the women to squeal appealingly. There was a white-sand beach beyond the Recreation Hall and wooden piers in the shape of an "H." The piers were for diving and no fishing was allowed, the fishermen sitting motionless as stumps around the edge of the lake, or casting from small outboard-motored boats. You could shoot pool on coin-operated tables in the Recreation Hall, or play checkers free, or eat very bad hamburgers on cold buns. Fortunately there was no Southern Fried Chicken of the kind that looks slick and mucusy when the crust falls off. No hoecake or buttermilk biscuits swimming in drippins. Just good old, regrettable Southern Fried Hamburgers with onions that hung out over your chin.

St. James and Crystal had ridden the Honda 500 to the park, and sat on the big veranda overlooking the lake waiting for Boles and his crew to finish setting up the shooting gallery and barbecue stand. The metal chairs with iron-mesh backs and seats were painted the peculiar mildew-blue that lawn furniture from Mexico is painted. But the chairs were comfortable, the view excellent. Crystal in olive-drab shorts and a matching T-shirt and sneakers was ravishing, but as yet unravished.

Sitting in identical chairs at a mildew-blue table near them was a middle-aged couple from Minnesota. It was easy to tell they were from Minnesota because the man said so. "We're from Minnesota," said the man, who was wearing L. L. Bean boating moccasins, a natty open-work cap, and a blue coverall. "You people live 'round here?"

"Yassuh," said St. James, hating himself for what he was about to do but knowing that either he had to do it or get up and leave.

"You really have the accent," said the woman. "I'd give anything to have an accent like that."

"Shucks, ma'am, I doan rightly know what you mean."

"You know, *Southern*, it's so *Southern*. I think this must be the most romantic place in the world." She turned to Crystal and smiled a really nice smile and said, "Are you and your Daddy on holiday?"

"It's Sunday," said Crystal.

"Oh." The woman appeared taken aback. "You don't talk like your father. I thought you were a Southern Belle."

"I'm from Colorado," said Crystal. St. James could tell she was furious with him. "What part of Minnesota are you from?"

"Near Duluth. We almost froze to death the past winter."

"I read about it—uh, I'm going inside a minute, can I bring you anything, maybe a Coke?"

"That would be nice, I'll go with you, and help you," said the woman.

"Fine." Crystal arose, looking down at St. James with loathing. Her legs were without blemish. A cool wind had erected her nipples beneath the olive-colored cotton.

When they were gone the man said that it was odd that Crystal did not have a Southern accent, that she was the way he'd always imagined a Southern Belle would look.

"Wa-al, suh, she been away to Sophie Newcomb School

119

in New Orleans. Come back for the Spring break a different kid. Las' Chrismas she was talkin' fine. She's bad to put on airs 'round strangers, anyway."

The man studied the lake for a time. "We just got here an hour ago and my wife loves it. You're making fun of us, aren't you? I tell you what, sport, you say anything to hurt my wife and you'll be sorry. If Lila wants to make something big out of this goddamn mudhoe I'll go along with it—and believe me, you better, too."

St. James was ashamed and flabbergasted. He'd been on the verge of saying that the scars on the bannister of the porch were where a Yankee soldier swung a saber at his old grandmammy. He was every bit as loony as Crystal on her looniest day; except that Crystal rarely had fun at someone else's expense.

"I'm sorry, sir," said St. James.

"It's okay," said the man, "probably something in the water."

Crystal and the lady with the nice smile appeared with the canned Cokes and the two couples sat together for almost a half hour, talking and looking at the young water skiers on the lake. The boat and skis opened up the green skin of the lake like a zipper, exposing an ever-widening "V" of white foam which finally melted into the water. The air smelled of cold, deep water and sunshine and pine and the trees glittered, their needles as glossy as if they had been shampooed. St. James said little. He sat simmering in shame. When he did speak he had no accent, no Southern accent at all.

Lila said nothing about his abrupt loss of ma'ams and yassuhs and when finally they parted she hugged them both and said she hoped they met again.

Crystal hung frost as thick as fur on him during the walk to the bike on the parking lot flanking the Recreation Building. He said wasn't it a splended day for the contests and she said yes, wasn't it. He said he didn't know what got into him to do anything in such poor taste as he'd done on the veranda. "The only excuse I can find," he said, "is that when I was in school the kids from the east wore better-looking clothes and they had more money and better-looking dates. And they treated me like a redneck." He watched her from the sides of his eyes to see if she was swallowing the garbage.

"Which you apparently were," she said.

"I guess so," he said, cranking the bike. She did not put her arms around him, but held instead onto the strap across the quilted vinyl seat.

"What you did a while ago," said Crystal, "was not simply a matter of poor taste."

"I apologized to the man."

"Those people were interested in you," said Crystal. "Lila said they'd been saving four years for this trip. You were a contemptible creep."

He knew it was true. There could be no valid alibi. Mostly he'd been trying to show off for her. Also he was angry that they mistook her for his daughter. Now the splendor drained out of the blue and gold day and it balled up in a lump and fell on his head. He tried to laugh it off but Crystal did not laugh; and her breasts did not touch his back.

At the north end of the two-hundred-acre lake in a blaze of red Japanese magnolias and pink-and-white dogwood Boles had set up his show, a concession stand, a dozen or so redwood tables, and a backdrop of stacked bales of hay for the targets. It had been decided to have no firearms competition, only slings and bows and crossbows. Boles explained that park regulations forbade the use of guns.

"Waddaya think, hoss?" Boles beamed. He wore an

121

apron over his green shirt and pants and there was a wobbly white chef's hat on his sweating head. "Here, keep turning these ribs for me on the grill."

"How do I know when to turn them?" St. James asked, looking around for Crystal who had disappeared in the swarm of people, cars, and campers.

"When they begin to stink," said Boles. "Or if they catch fire." He had a flitgun filled with water in case of emergency. There was a gallon jug of barbecue sauce for basting the roasting meat. "I got to check the weapons on the tables."

"You mean yours—the stuff you brought?"

"Sure, and a lot of the people have items on the tables, everything from Civil War hoss pistols to an old Sharps rifle, a buffalo gun. They must be twenty thousand bucks worth a stuff on them tables." Boles loved guns. Any kind of gun, from water pistols to field artillery. He was an incurable collector, and it was probable, if not inevitable, that before the day was done he'd manage a few trades or purchases, or both. Boles would interrupt almost anything to examine a gun, and now that he was squarely in the midst of hundreds of revolvers, rifles, and shotguns he seemed stunned with surfeit. A pink-faced tomcat in a rat factory.

"Orson, you don't have half enough meat here to feed these people."

"At six dollars a throw?"

"They won't pay that."

"Then we got plenty—quit *worrying*. You seen any red Datsuns or anybody wearing a shepherd's bag?"

"Not yet."

"Don't start hawkin' ribs until the contests're over—that way they can't eat and run. The icebox yonder is full a ice-cold orange and Pepsi, a buck a throw."

"They can buy them for fifty cents at the Recreation Building."

"People's thirsty and lazy, hoss. See you in a while."

The wall of hay bales with archery targets pinned to it was at the bottom of a slope, almost at the edge of the lake. At the upper end of the slope, in the concession area, St. James had a view of both the display tables and the shooters. Boles was busy distributing bows and quivers to contestants and Crystal was helping him. She did not look at the concession stand, but even at a distance she looked smooth and graceful, all of a piece. The slingshot competition was scheduled as a finale.

St. James sold the cans of soft drinks for a half-dollar and kept turning the meat until he was bored with it and he put out the fire, dousing embers with the spray can of water. He stood there in the stream staring down the slope at Crystal and wondering if he had doused her embers as well. Permanently. Crystal could be very touchy with clods. Yassuh. The outrageous did not faze her if it was imaginative. In fact she doted on the outrageous. But Crystal could not abide clods.

He felt sad there in the booth with the wet muck and the meat. Alone with his recrimination, he felt little surprise to see Lila Winn accepting an umbrella and a beach towel from Boles. Mr. Winn stood by. This would really complete their odyssey. A yellow umbrella and a beach towel. In Boles's ads in the paper he'd stated the winners would receive nice surprises.

The archery competition was scheduled to be divided into three divisions: men, women, and minors. When the men began shooting, St. James saw Crystal talking to Boles and then she started walking up the long slope toward the booth, the curtain of heavy blonde hair swinging in sunlight just the way hair swung in the TV commercials. Her legs were lightly tanned, and glossy knees seemed to blink when she walked.

When she arrived at the booth she rested her elbows on the counter and gave him a level look. "Orson wants you to come down when the slingshooting begins. He says he needs you."

"When will that be?"

"Soon. There aren't many people interested in the archery."

"I can't believe Lila won the women's. She looks so frail and indoorsy."

"She was the only woman in the women's division," said Crystal. "You want to make something funny out of that."

"No." He didn't want to make something funny out of anything for a long time.

"Good, come on down when you see us setting up the bottles."

"What about the meat?"

"I don't know," said Crystal. "Throw it away, eat it, I don't care."

When she left he went to the grill where the sauce-soaked roasted ribs were stacked on the metal rack above the sodden cinders. He lifted a sheet of ribs and tore off three or four and found some soft white rolls in a cellophane pack. Suddenly he was famished. He opened a can of Pepsi and had himself a feast on the greasy red meat and fresh bread.

Then he saw them taking down the archery targets and setting up the empty bottles. St. James wiped his chin and hands on an apron that was hanging on the side of the grill; belching barbecue sauce he let himself out of the booth and started down the slope. He felt much better. About everything. But he still expected no revelations from the slingshot competition. There seemed to be six children to every adult in the crowd, and many of them would be smearing themselves with Solarcaine tonight. Their squeals rolled out across the glittering lake and they swirled and hopped about on the slope and among the cars and other vehicles on the asphalt lot adjacent to the contest area. Someone had a huge St. Bernard which appeared as excited as the kids and it ran barking to the water's edge and yelped at the water skiers, lobster red and erect as they zippered open the cold water, waving at the people on the shore.

It was a hell of a nice day.

He would apologize again to the Winns.

A dozen rubber-powered slingshots and Boles's own weapon of rawhide thongs and leather pocket were laid out on a table half-covered with pistols, most of these compact derringers, the celebrated sleevegun of Mississippi riverboat gamblers. Several of the competitors had brought their own slingshots. Others were picking over items on the table, hefting them for weight and balance and for rubber-snap. There was a little brown basket filled with marbles for ammunition and scattered about on top of the marbles were a score or so of the nougat-shaped pieces of quartzite that Boles had pried loose from the roof of the Mobley after plaster casts were made of cavities in the tar. The white stones, frosted on the outside, looked like clear glass inside. This you could see in the broken ones. There were very narrow bands of ziggy bright brown in some, so that the combined shape and coloration made them quite distinctive. A few had tar stuck to them, but most did not, showing only smudges where they had been fastened to the roof.

Boles said, "It might seem silly to you, but they's a chance somebody will choose the rocks and the rawhide sling. Help me keep an eye. I told Miss Crystal. I want

125

to know even if somebody just picks up a rock and gives it a funny look."

"They'll all choose the marbles and the rubber," said St. James.

He began sifting the throng with his eyes, looking for the Winns so he could be done with his penance. He saw Rudell Link, the deceased mayor's snowy-toothed son, dragging a couple of little kids toward the lake. Then Elwood doing the same thing. John Trask was among those present, and he was talking to Dillard Harmon and Stephanie in the dappled shade of a flowering dogwood, the three of them laughing and you could see through Stephanie's flame-colored skirt.

A towheaded boy maybe ten years old with a tired, smeary face, wearing shorts he had to keep pulling out of his crack, asked St. James, "What time's the barbecue ready?"

"It's cooked."

"When they serve the stuff?"

"After the slingshooting. You hungry?"

"Yessir. I didn't have no breakfast—you know what the barbecue's going to cost? I mean three or four ribs?"

"They tell me six dollars."

"Jesus, mister."

"I agree. You go on up to the booth, there's a door on the left end of it, you just help yourself—but don't go crazy."

"I ain't got no six dollars."

"It's on me." St. James felt a fine glow of decency, which he needed, because he could not locate the Winns for a proper, full-bloomed apology.

The boy whooped and leaped high in the air. He stank of insect repellent and his legs were covered with what looked to be scratched ant-bites. "You mean it, mister?"

"I mean it."

The kid took off up the slope as fast as his dirty, bitten legs would carry him. St. James watched him until he disappeared inside the booth, saw his head and shoulders through the open front of the booth, which had a counter and a wall that ended about four feet off the ground. The top half of the front wall was propped open on its hinges with a long stick. It was getting very hot. During the night the temperature dropped into the forties, but now it was like summertime.

Soon the boy came running back down the slope to St. James. "They's a dog as big as a calf in there," he yelled. "He's eat 'em all and what he hasn't eat he's slobbering on."

St. James remembered the St. Bernard yelping at the water skiers on the lake. "I'm sorry, son," he said, reaching into his pocket for a couple of dollars. "Take this and go that way to the Recreation Building and get you a hamburger and a cold drink."

"I wanted some barbecue," the boy said, taking the money. "I had my mouth set for some a them barbecue ribs."

"They were greasy, son."

"I ain't your goddamn son," said the boy trotting off toward the Recreation Building.

Boles, still wearing the trembling chef's hat and an apron imprinted on the chest with BAMA'S BEST, was in high good humor as he explained the rules to prospective contestants.

"As you can see, the bottles is numbered and you got to sing out the number you shooting at. Accidents don't count."

Snaggering from the crowd. Sound of a speeding motorboat far down at the opposite end of the kidney-shaped lake, the noise only a light snoring.

"If you call out number three and you hit some other number Miss Crystal will replace what you broke but no cigar. Zat clear?"

The contestants nodded, slingshots dangling from eager fists. Most of them were teen-aged boys, only a few men, one of whom was Rudell, now unencumbered by the fruit of his loins. On the edge of the crescent formed by the contestants St. James saw a man who looked like Robert Goodbee except that his face was clean and he wore a white long-sleeved shirt and dark slacks with creases. Wisps of gray hair combed like guitar strings over a sunburned dome. Narrow eyes. When he moved to get closer to Boles he hobbled like Goodbee. Hell, it couldn't be. He had a slingshot in his left hand.

"We put the bottles here in front a the bales to catch any wild shots," Boles said reasonantly in country-preacher's voice. He grinned and waved his hands at the water. "Worst harm you can do is sink one a them dudes out there on the skis."

General laughter and hooting from the crowd.

Boles consulted his notes: these were clipped to a varnished board. "Each contestant gets ten shots. The one that breaks the most bottles wins. If there's a tie we'll have a shootoff. Is that clear, neighbors?"

Murmured agreement from the shooters.

"All right, Mister Robert Goodbee."

Goodbee held up his slingshot and stepped onto the firing line and Boles, in the interest of showmanship, with his chronic disregard for some forms of logic, sang out: "Ready on the right . . . rrr-rrr-r-ready on the left . . . com-mence fi-reeng . . ."

Goodbee made a gurgling sound through the hidden

hole in his chest. He held up four fingers signifying choice of targets. Then he busted the hell out of the bottle marked "4."

Boles bent to his clipboard and scribbled into the record. He straightened and sang out: "When you rr-rrr-ready, suh, fire at will . . ."

Goodbee held up three fingers and promptly shattered the third bottle from the left of a line of ten bottles. He gripped the handle of the slingshot in his left hand and with the right he drew the pocket to the tip of his nose, left arm locked rigidly but shaking badly.

The old man then missed eight shots in a row.

Boles came to St. James and hissed: "What was he shootin', the marbles or rocks?"

"I wasn't watching him when he put the stuff in his pocket."

"You dumbass, you know what?"

"What?"

"I didn't watch neither."

Crystal said from behind St. James: "He fired rocks on the first two targets, then switched to the marbles. I saw him loading his pocket a while ago."

"What about Rudell?" said Boles.

"All rocks and he's got the rawhide sling," said Crystal.

Boles appeared pleased. He did not know that the St. Bernard had gobbled up BAMA'S BEST in the barbecue booth. "Fine," he said, his white hat quivering. He returned to his post and called out the name of the mayor's son who now was slipping his middle finger through the loop of one thong and pinching the thick clump of knots in the other thong between his thumb and forefinger.

The boy whom St. James had given the two dollars

appeared at Boles's elbow as he prepared to chant his firing signals. "You said we was going to have barbecue," the boy piped.

"Not now, boy, I'm busy."

St. James stepped forward and took the boy by the arm, drawing him away. "You let go a me," the kid howled.

"Git out a here you little shitass," Boles hissed. Then smiling benevolently he went into his act, the crowd clapping in anticipation, fathers holding babies high so they could see.

The mayor's son Rudell turned slightly sideways and began whipping the rock round and round in a circle like a man getting ready to crack a bullwhip. On about the fourth round he turned loose of the knotted thong and the rock sang out over the hay bales and began skipping on the water. It traveled an incredible distance, almost a quarter of the width of the lake. Wherever it struck the water little popcorn balls of foam burped up.

Rudell shook his head and got set for the second shot, which struck the bales but did not break a bottle. The St. Bernard gallumped onto the scene, moving slowly, its muzzle scarlet with barbecue sauce. It lay down on the slope between the firing line and the targets, closing its eyes. With a contented shudder it fell asleep. Someone whistled but the dog did not stir.

Firing rocks directly over the sleeping dog Rudell broke four bottles, one by accident, the others called shots.

He loaded the leather sling again and slowly commenced the whirling, each round of the rock faster than the one before. Boles was standing out of the line of fire, about midway between targets and the slingshot, gazing down moist cheeks at figures on the clipboard. St. James could have sworn that Rudell Link was watching the captain of detectives. With only a minor adjustment in stance the shooter could send the rock whizzing into Boles's head. St. James opened his mouth to cry out as the shooter's feet shifted slightly, but it was too late and the rawhide whip cracked the rock over the bales and into the lake, narrowly missing a startled water skier. Then Rudell without change of stance put three more stones in the lake. Still, it seemed to St. James, the shooter was watching Boles, whipping the rocks very high so that they did not skip when they landed.

Rudell then showed the crowd his basketful of white teeth, wound the rawhide strips around his hand after removing his finger from the loop. He walked over toward the table and underhanded tossed the balled sling onto the redwood. The crowd gave him a reverberating ovation. He turned smiling to survey his admirers, then held up a fist and walked away toward the parking area. Evidently he had no interest in winning the umbrella and beach towel.

St. James sat down with a thump of the new grass, scooping up a handful of brown pine needles and holding them under his nose, foolishly sniffing at them as if he expected to find strength in the fragrance. He envisioned the stone blurring from the sling to embed itself in the temple an inch below the line of the white hat.

John Trask, the motorcycle magnate, did not compete, and Boles found this disappointing. The detective registered no undue excitement when he learned the sleeping dog had eaten the ribs. He was not happy about it, but did not raise much of a fuss. Only an obligatory curse word or two and a malevolent glare at the St. Bernard. "Maybe it was dog meat," said Boles. "It didn't smell all that great, did it?"

"Nope."

Boles's heavy pink face lit up and he said, "Maybe the sonofabitch won't never git up from there."

The remainder of the slingshot event seemed to last forever. No one else used the primitive thongs or rocks. The contest was limited to males and it was won by a seventh-grader from Holly Springs who brought his own shooter, which consisted of pink rubber and the whittled fork of a sycamore branch. He made five called shots. He looked as if he was going to laugh when Boles presented him the prizes.

Crystal and St. James helped Boles clean up the greasy shambles on the floor of the booth. The place was a wreck, the barbecue grill overturned and meat and bones and Parker House rolls covering the floor of the concession stand. The booth buzzed with flies of several kinds, huge horseflies, ordinary houseflies, and blue-bottle flies. The big ones bit. Boles slapped a bare forearm as he squatted, scraping bones onto a soiled towel. "Those damn things got teeth like a dog," he said. His green shirt was soaked with sweat. "What you think, hoss? You think the show was worth the trouble."

St. James said yes and he told Boles about Rudell. "I was afraid there for a minute he was going to zonk you. I know he wasn't looking at the target. Looked to me like he'd found your Sweet Spot."

"Sweet Spot?"

St. James then told them what Briscoe Risk had said about Elwood kissing the baby and all three of them were convulsed, laughing much more than the thing deserved. In any case there was a lessening of tension and Crystal was on the thaw. She had a pretty laugh. She had a pretty everything and even in bright sunlight you couldn't see anything that wasn't altogether marvelous. She was dropping ribs into a tattered straw hat she'd found outside the booth.

"No one acted funny about the rocks," she said to Boles. "If they were suspicious it didn't show."

"Only Goodbee and Rudell used the stones off the top of the Mobley," said St. James.

"That doesn't mean anything one way or the other, hoss. We know that the rocks that we dug out of the mayor and commissioner came off the bank roof. We've put a micrometer to the plaster casts and the rocks and the match is near-perfect. But we don't have any idea *why*, with a skitter of gravel all over the county, the killer chose those rocks, or whether he even noticed that the ones we mixed in with the marbles came off the bank." Boles was completely serious, squatting there in the booth with a pawful of rib bones, swatting at the flies. "I want to get with you later, hoss, and go over all this."

"Fine."

St. James stood up and saw that most of the people were gone and the St. Bernard was no longer asleep on the slope. He heard the drone of a boat motor and as he watched a young skier appeared at the end of a long tow-rope zinging along behind a red-and-white boat on the skin of the lake. Robert Goodbee was hobbling along the water's edge. Suddenly the boat curved toward the shore in an arc, its prow lifting in the turn, and the skier turned loose of the rope and rode into the shallows.

The youth removed the skis and put them on his shoulders and splashed up out of the lake to join Goodbee. They stood there on the edge of the lake, apparently engaged in earnest conversation, Goodbee's hand spread against his white shirt near the base of his throat. The skier at one point shook his head violently and half-

133

turning stomped a bare foot against the grass. Then they walked diagonally up the slope toward the parking lot, disappearing in the dogwood and pines and Japanese magnolias.

"What you see, hoss?" Boles said, still plopping bones onto the filthy towel.

St. James told him.

"Git on up to the parking lot and see what they driving."

"You have three men up there, Orson."

"Never mind that, go look."

"I'll go with you," Crystal said.

She held his hand as they walked under the trees on a cushion of slippery pine needles and although they said nothing the feeling between them was good. St. James wanted to stop and take her in his arms, but he thought of the Minnesota couple and how they'd believed he was Crystal's father. Further, he hoped to reach the lot in time to see Goodbee and the youth, who very well could be the mysterious "grandson" who'd shot the rats for the stew.

Or had he?

The old man had handled the sling with authority during the contest. That is, on the first two shots. Perhaps he'd deliberately missed the others. There was no question but that Rudell Link had quit trying after smashing a few bottles. He wasn't a dummy. He didn't want to look too good. Had he really been tempted to put the crunch on Boles right there before a hundred or so spectators and kibitzers? No one could have proved it wasn't an accident—that he'd not simply turned loose of the knotted thong at the wrong instant.

There were still three cars and two pickup trucks on the parking lot.

But Goodbee and the youth were not there. A quarter-mile distant, at the end of the lake St. James saw a red sports car crossing the concrete spillway heading for the park exit. He pointed the car out to Crystal. She said she didn't think it was a Datsun.

17

THEY HAD PUT THE TRAPDOOR LID BACK OVER THE HOLE and Crystal was standing on it, her back arched, hands in her hair. The trapdoor lid fitted over a frame of two-by-fours like the lid on a box of candy and Crystal did a slow, swaying shuffle-step on the painted tin. He could barely see her from six feet away where he sat on the waist-high parapet. The concrete stung his behind through thin poplin slacks and the wind from the river was cool, almost cold, against his back. Crystal was feeling sexy.

What are you thinking about?" she whispered.

"Not *that*."

"Not what?"

"You know," said St. James. "You know damned well."

The night sky was heavy with thready banks of clouds, greasy-looking drifts which covered the moon for minutes. They rubbed over the face of the moon polishing it briefly to cover it again.

"Just hold me," said Crystal.

Against his better judgment he hopped off the parapet and went to her and put his arms around her. Despite her slimness, if there was a single word for her it was "round." Her waist was round. Her arms and legs round, her breasts and shoulders. Buttocks and neck. Warm and smooth and round and electric, he thought, remembering the day she said the squirrels were electric. Imagine being able to run headfirst down a tree, she'd said.

"Crystal you know why we came up here."

"I still think it's silly, Kiel, the killer isn't about to come. Orson discontinued his stakeout a week ago." She was kissing his chin and her flat belly rotated against him and he felt the hardening against her. "Come on," he said. "Stop the shit."

"You're being mean."

"All contemptible creeps are mean. Come on, over behind that thing." He stepped off the trapdoor and they moved around a couple of ventilators with sheet-metal coolie hats. He held her wrist and extended his free hand in front of him. When he touched the metal wall of the structure housing the elevator, cable pulleys, and machinery he pulled her along behind him until they had the little building between them and the trapdoor.

"You still haven't explained why you think anything will come of this," Crystal said.

"Maybe nothing will," St. James said. "Maybe we don't have much in the way of odds, or even logic. Holding a winning lottery ticket isn't logical either; but every time there's a drawing there's a winner."

She was on her knees on the tarred gravel and it was pitch-black behind the wall. He said, "The loony who killed the mayor and commissioner will come back here. Don't laugh. I know he will. He killed twice and each time he used a stone from this damned roof, right?"

She got to her feet and put her arms around him. "So

why does he have to come up here for one of his silly rocks? Orson had plenty of them at the contest this afternoon."

"Right, he had twenty, plus the marbles. Goodbee fired two of them and Rudell ten. That's twelve, right?"

"I love your brain."

"Shut up. We counted the ones left, or rather Orson did and there were eight."

"Golleee-ee-eee," Crystal whispered.

"So nobody took any home with them, right?"

"How do you know Little David didn't fill his pockets when he was up here the first time?"

"Because we checked every inch of this dumb roof— and far's we could find, only two rocks were pried out of the tar."

"*Bo-reeng,*" said Crystal.

"It may be boring, but it's the truth. Now goddammit behave yourself. And be quiet."

"How do you know he's coming *tonight?*"

"I don't."

"Well why're we here?"

"Don't you ever just *feel* something?"

"Of course," said Crystal, giggling. "You ought to know that."

The double doors on the ground floor of the Mobley Bank Building were made of glass framed in heavy bronze. Always locked at night, the doors opened into a marble-sheathed foyer at the far end of which were the two elevators, these self-operating after the attendants knocked off. The banking operation was to the left of the foyer and it had doors identical to those in the face of the ten-storied building.

People who had offices in the upper stories owned keys to the front door—architects, doctors, dentists, and insurance firms. At least half the office space in the Mobley was vacant and it was hoped that if the city council ever managed to "revitalize" the heart of the old business district the Mobley, too, would come to life. The Chamber of Commerce had a sprawling suite of offices on the third floor and St. James had borrowed a key from Paul Ott, the salaried director of the chamber, a skinny native of Kentucky who generally was out of town on what he called "industry-hunting junkets." Ott was a hog for any kind of publicity for Catherine, and St. James told him he wanted to get some nighttime photos of the city—that later Crystal would photograph Ott and other chamber dignitaries and run this along with a full-page revitalization feature.

But—could the killer get in at night?

Crystal, as if reading St. James's thoughts, said: "Doesn't Rudell have his law offices here?"

"Yes."

"I think he's creepy, *really* creepy. The way he looked whipping those rocks around his head . . . you *hear* something?"

He straightened and she tightened her arms around his waist. His chin was on top of her head. She smelled of Rolos and shampoo. He heard nothing but the wind whispering in the ventilators, and they stood there listening.

St. James freed himself and edged around the corner of the elevator pulley-housing but he could make out nothing, not even the lid of the trapdoor. Faint glow of moonlight leaking along the scalloped edge of a cloud, then almost total blackness. Smell of water from the river four blocks away. Smell of tar from the roof. Smell of Rolos and Prell and raspberry lipstick.

"Don't you *hear* that?" Crystal whispered. One of the most irritating things about her was that she invariably

139

could hear and see things better than he. When they were on the road she could read signs ahead before he even saw them. When they were at work she heard fire-truck sirens a mile away, fainter than the singing of a mosquito. *"Lis-sen, now,"* her chin against his shoulder blade.

"I hear it," he whispered. A soft scraping, followed by a thump.

A car passed in the street, its radio blaring the unmistakable music of Boy George and Culture Club. It was somehow reassuring, this testimony of other life on the planet. A girl squealed down there, the sound very clear, the age-old don't-put-that-frog-down-my-back squeal. An oh-you-naughty-thing squeal. And then the noise was gone.

Poking his head around the corner St. James could make out vaguely a dark form emerging from the open trapdoor, noiselessly and without haste. It moved off parallel with the parapet and he heard the feet on the gravel. Moonlight flickered dimly for a moment in the windy blackness and he saw, or thought he saw, the figure kneeling or stooping thirty feet away near a ventilator. For the first time it occurred to him that coming up here without a police backup was not altogether the brightest thing he'd ever done.

"You see him?" Crystal whispered. "My God, Kiel, he's twenty-five feet tall; what's he doing?"

"Hush, I don't know."

There was a screaking, as of steel on stone. "Be still," St. James said. "He'll hear your feet on the gravel." She was wearing her fuck-me boots with the thick leather soles, a poor choice for this kind of assignment.

"You hear that?" she said as the screaking continued. "My God, he's got a knife."

"You don't know that."

"Do you have a knife?" she whispered.

140

"I don't even have a safety pin." He reached behind him and nudged her backward farther into the shelter of the pulley-housing. During his daytime visit he had seen some lengths of lead tubing lying along the rear wall of the little building, stuff apparently discarded by electricians. He stooped and felt along the wall until his fingers felt the open end of one of the insulation tubes and, sticking a finger in the hole, he lifted it; but it was much too long for use as a weapon. He knew that there were shorter lengths, but he tried three and each seemed longer than the other.

"What are you *doing*?" Crystal sounded scared.

The screaking stopped.

Was he listening?

Had he heard them?

St. James held an end of the tubing in his right hand and with his left he pushed down. The stuff bent readily, about four feet from the end. He worked the bend back and forth until finally it snapped, the longer portion falling with a leaden bump against gravel.

"Who's there?" a voice called.

St. James and Crystal stood frozen, backs against the brick.

"Come out a there!"

"You stay put, kid," St. James said to Crystal. "Keep your cover." And as the moon came sliding across between clouds he stepped out onto open roof holding his club against his chest with both fists and seeing then the glint of the blade and the figure of the man standing spraddle-legged, waiting. Saying nothing, simply waiting there with the long slice of steel in his hand, it catching moonlight in crawling spiders of light.

"You ought to put that thing away," said St. James. "You liable to cut somebody."

No answer, only the hissing of April wind in the ven-

141

tilators and the muttering of a passing car ten stories below in the almost deserted street. Little moonlight now and neither man moving to close the space between them. And St. James thought: Is this the way it's going to end? Is this the ultimate deadline? A knife in your guts on a roof a hundred feet above a dying street, the smell of the river in your nose and about to piss in your pants?

"We figured it was about time you showed," he said conversationally. "You knew they'd pulled the stakeout, heh?"

Not a word from the indistinct, waiting figure.

"Heh, cat got your tongue?" St. James was amazed that his voice was steady. Somewhere in the surge of fear, in the swirl of thoughts and sensations, he was able to listen to himself, to the soft, steady words, as if they were coming from someone else.

But he couldn't just stand there with jumping muscles, adrenalin incinerating his brain. Standing still was impossible and he damned well could not retreat. Hoping to God that it was true that the best defense was a good offense he moved forward, now swinging the section of lead tubing at his side, then raising it high as the figure moved to the far side of the waist-high ventilator.

"I don't want trouble with you, Buster," St. James said. "You put away the blade and I'll get rid a this thing."

No response, the dark faceless figure moving from side to side, like a kid standing up in the back of a car rocking from foot to foot. St. James felt suddenly faint and dizzy and he reached out with his left hand to steady himself against the parapet and as he did so the wispy moonlight vanished into total blackout and he heard a swift scrabbling of feet against gravel, felt the impact of the hurtling body, heard Crystal's scream.

Where was his club?

142

Where was the goddamned club?

The raw concrete edge of the parapet cut into the small of his back and the man had some kind of grip on his face, clawing, arching him backward over the parapet. St. James flailed out fists and seemed to hit nothing vulnerable, only elbows and skull. He managed finally to seize a wrist and dislodge the grip on his face, the gouging fingers. He could see nothing at all now and the pain in his eyes was almost paralyzing; so that when the knife came he knew what it was, knew that he was cut, but it hurt less than the other. He felt the wetness and warmth of the blood and then there was a forearm beneath his chin, hard against the Adam's apple, forcing him back and out. He tried to throw punches, but there was nothing to throw with, no gas in the tank; yet he kept trying, as if in a bad dream where someone has melted your bones and you swing noodles at the devil. The knife hit him a second time. It really wasn't bad at all the second time. He opened torn lids as wide as he could but could not make out the face of the man. St. James's arms were simply flapping as he tried to defend himself. His last thought was to wonder what would happen to Crystal and then he wondered what he would look like on the brick of the ancient street. Would he splatter? He had once seen a fellow paratrooper after a parachute malfunction at Fort Benning, the trooper's carbine a crescent against his broken belly and when they rolled him onto a tarpaulin he was strawberry Jello inside his fatigues. Flap-flap went St. James's arms, flap-flap-flap.

18

WHEN HE REGAINED CONSCIOUSNESS THE MOON WAS AL-
most as bright as daylight and he lay on his back in the
gravel at the base of the parapet. He called out weakly
for Crystal and there was no answer.

He knew that she was dead.

He touched his torn face, which was sticky with blood,
and the ribs on the right side where his shirt was stuck
to him.

Get up, he said to himself. Get up and find her. She
would be behind the elevator building, whatever was
left of her. No more Crystal. "I love you, kid," he said
to the moon, which expanded and shrank, and reap-
peared as big as one of those silvery spherical tanks you
see at refineries. "Dear God, don't let her be dead," he
said to the moon and then he was crying, racked by sobs
which jerked his belly against his spine, ripped at his
ribs.

Just before he lost consciousness he heard the mosquito
song of the siren faraway at the north end of town.

He did not hear its expanding scream as it approached,

nor the voices below as ambulance attendants piled out, Boles shouting at them to hurry.

Oblivious now, St. James dreamed of Crystal in the baptismal tank and he was holding her and there was a blinding light that raised smoke from the green water. Crystal's face was slashed, but she was smiling and a great rumbling voce said, "Behold my children in whom I am well pleased. Go ahead and screw her, son."

And St. James said, "Not in your tank, sir."

And Crystal said, still smiling, "Do it, Kiel." The blood from her face dripped into the clear green water.

In the stained-glass window high above the water Robert Goodbee, radiant in the light, was breathing through the hole in his chest, his rag billowing with each breath. He held a shepherd's staff and he said, "I shall feed your flesh to the fowls of the air and the beasts of the field."

19

~~~~~~

"WHAT ABOUT HIS EYES, HIS POOR EYES?" HE HEARD Crystal say.

And then a voice he did not recognize: "No real damage there, most of it superficial—the ointment will keep down infection until the tissue heals. He's lost a great deal of blood but the knife missed his lung."

"He looks so pitiful," Crystal said, tears in her voice.

"He'll be good as new, Miss Bunt."

And then Boles's voice, not sounding much like Boles, yet like no one else; it couldn't be anyone else. "I shouldn't've let him go up there without one a my men."

"Well," said Crystal. "I like *that*."

"You know what I mean, Miss Crystal, you both could a been killed. You were lucky."

St. James opened his eyes and saw the bottle of whole blood hanging from its tree over the head of the bed. He tried to wink at Boles but there was a red-hot cuckleburr in his eye and it hurt when he breathed. "This is lucky?" he said.

Crystal laid a cool hand on his head. "Be still," she said. "You be still."

His head felt as if someone had been using it for a bowling ball and had pumped it full of killer bees. They buzzed when he turned his head to look at Crystal. "You," he said. "You." Her face was not cut and her arms and shoulders, bare and round, were unmarked. "I love you Kiel, I love you so much," she said, bending over him so that the curtain of hair fell over his bandaged face, he smelling the sweetness of her, his torn lips against her skin.

"I wouldn't do that, Miss," said the doctor. "Infection, you know."

"Fuck the infection," said St. James, trying to reach for her and draw her back.

"Behave, darling," said Crystal. "You're going to be fine, if you behave—the doctor's right."

"Did you get the guy?" St. James said to Boles. "Did you nail the sonofabitch?"

"No, but he's got a hell of a headache."

"I clobbered him," said Crystal. "I used the other half of that piece of pipe and I beat his head like a drum."

"I thought you were dead," said St. James. "I knew you were dead." The bottle of whole blood, looking big enough to fill an elephant, seemed to swing on the iron stanchion. He watched it swing and shrink and grow and swing. It was the color of mulberries. He could not hold his eyes open against the pain. He slept.

Several times during the night he roused briefly, not trying to open his eyes, which were stuck tight, but hearing movement near the bed, smelling Prell and raspberry, but no Rolos.

Once he heard the crackling of nurse-starch and the

squeaking of rubber-soled shoes and felt a needle's sting. The rough cold touch of the rubbing alcohol on his arm. "Don't roll onto your bad side," someone said. "It's full of stitches."

Nine days later when they turned him loose he was a wiser man. He had learned the value of being able to blink his eyes. He had learned also the rich pleasure of being able to breathe a full breath of air, plain old, free air. He and Crystal had learned, too, that Ernest Hemingway must have been kidding when he wrote of sex between a wounded man and a healthy young woman in a hospital bed. It was not feasible—or even bearable. The libido did not thrive on pain.

Between Crystal and Boles he learned what there was to know about what happened on the roof and about developments in the police investigation. Crystal said that when she screamed and came running out from behind her shelter, she forgot to arm herself—and had to scuttle back to get the length of electrical conduit for a club; that there was enough moonlight for her to swat the man where it would do him the least good, her first shot catching him on the nape of the neck and when he pivoted she let him have it full in the face, a face that looked to have some kind of covering over it. Then she hit him in the head, three times. "He went to his knees and I heard the knife clatter on the gravel. I thought I'd killed him. I hoped I'd killed him. When he turned loose of you you slid down off the parapet like a sack of meal."

"Come on, kid, not a goddamned sack of meal. Jazz it up, make it a sack of shit. Or let me slide down like a wounded hero."

"All right," said Crystal. "A sack of shit. While I was trying to attend to you he got to his feet and you wouldn't believe the way he moved. It was like I never hit him at all. He jumped in that hole in the roof and I don't believe he touched a single rung on the ladder."

After she made sure St. James was breathing she phoned Boles and returned with him to the scene. "You would a been proud of her, hoss," said Boles. "They isn't many women like that anymore."

"He only needs one," said Crystal.

Boles said he had gotten several clear prints off the bone handle of the Case jackknife. He showed St. James the knife, a mean-looking one-bladed thing, the blade about four inches long. It looked strangely familiar to St. James. He had the distinct feeling he had seen it before, but, raking his memory, he could not find a peg for it.

The captain of detectives said that, although the prints lifted were satisfactory, at this point there was nothing to compare them with. Goodbee had not been finger-printed, nor had the surly mechanic Dillard Harmon, nor Johnny Trask, the disgruntled would-be politician who operated the motorcycle agency. Nor Rudell Link, who in Boles's opinion also was a prime suspect.

"What you waiting for?" St. James wanted to know.

"Keep your britches on, hoss. We'll do what needs to be done."

I'm beginning to wonder."

"He'll be better when he gets the taste of hospital food out of his mouth," Boles said to Crystal. "We been through all this before. He turns plumb nasty on a balanced diet." Boles obviously referred to the Robinson murder a couple of years ago when St. James lost an ear-lobe and almost bought the farm in an unexpected showdown with a wild woman toting a 30-30 deer rifle.

"How come you never show up until I begin bleeding, Orson?"

"It's my nature, hoss, I'm a profesional, not a dumb-ass bleeder."

"Sure."

"An' I don't like hoggin' the limelight."

Crystal helped St. James into his windbreaker and Boles got on the phone and called the nurses' station and said Room 202 was ready to depart the premises. There was conversation about Blue Cross–Blue Shield after Boles handed the phone to St. James. When the hospital was satisfied in this regard the nurse on duty said she would send a wheelchair down the corridor to pick him up and take him down to his car.

"I don't need a wheelchair," he said.

"I'm sorry, it's the rules."

"They're going to roll me out," St. James said to Boles and Crystal. "It's the rules. I guess they don't want to be responsible for anybody falling on their head between here and the ride home."

"So let 'em roll you," said Boles. "Take everything you can get. God knows, you'll pay for it."

20

HE WAS THE LION OF THE NEWSROOM HIS FIRST MORNING
back on the job. The kids in sports appeared especially
impressed with his derring-do and they no longer leered
at Crystal. Brenda Keeton was almost absurdly respectful
to both St. James and Crystal because the two of them
had fed her enough information to keep her on page one
more than a week.

But lions are short-lived in the newsroom of a daily
newspaper, where reputations are made and shattered
between the first and final editions and the disciplined
hysteria needed to live beneath the sword of deadline
sometimes becomes less than controlled. Old enmities
flare and ancient resentments boil out of the turmoil. In
the afternoon he lost five local stories in The System. The
stories, one of them Brenda Keeton's piece on current
fingerprinting activities at the Regional Law Enforce-
ment Complex, was absolutely essential for the final edition.

"Where is the damned thing?" Brenda whined.

151

"I don't know," said St. James.

He had, with good reason, distrusted the video display terminals since their installation by the Southeastern Newspaper Alliance. The things simply swallowed things whole, items vanishing by the dozen. They could not be called up onto the screens of the word processors for editing. You could not go into the memory-bank room and look into the metal box. There was nothing to look into.

"Don't *do* this to me," Brenda said. "Don't *do* this again."

"I don't do it for Godsake. *I* don't swallow your crummy stories."

He stared at the clock on the wall. The clock was his antagonist. The clock ate him alive fifty weeks out of the year. The clock had frosted his hair and loosened his dewlaps; it had devoured his hopes for a better world. Always the clock. The round, white face was to the newsman what Dracula was to an innocent maiden wandering among the caskets in Transylvania: unrelenting, ravenous, immutable. The thing scissored away your life, day by day making a poorer man of you.

"So my stories are *crummy*?" said Brenda.

St. James inhaled deeply, his ribs aching only slightly. He could feel the line of little purple holes where the stitches had been. "I didn't mean that, honey, everything's going to be all right."

The remarkable thing was that he was telling the truth to her. Out of a clear sky the electronic system produced the missing items. Where had they been? Who the hell knew? Did they hide among the transistors and silicon chips, sulking there until your despair aroused some cold, amused response? Sometimes an expert had to be flown in from Hillendale, California, a disgustingly learned young man who spoke the computer-age language in a

152

patronizing tone of voice. He was actually able to take the metal shields off the kinky, sparkling guts of the computers and set things to right.

In any event, by the time the final reached the streets of Catherine, St. James had reestablished himself under the old banner, that of city editor and resident asshole. He had even talked ugly to the gawking kids in sports, who also lost several late-breaking stories in the computer.

St. James was up to his elbows in unopened mail when Crystal came to his desk and asked if he was all right.

"Why do you ask?" he said.

"I just wondered."

"Well don't wonder. I don't pay you to wonder."

He was truly back to form.

One nice thing happened. Kenny the executive editor returned from vacation. He had spent his three weeks off at a religious retreat on the Gulf Coast and he was radiant with faith and hope and all the goodies denied the average small-town newsman.

Kenny loved people and people loved Kenny. The staff, except for Barney, the sports editor, almost worshipped this pudgy whirlwind who was built like a bowling pin and had the energy of a laser.

The first thing Kenny did when he got back was to polish up his ceramic statuette of John the Baptist. "My gosh," he said to St. James. "I wish you would *look* at the dust on this desk." He said the retreat at the woodland camp on the coast had been a tonic and that several people from Catherine attended, including Alfred Deason, the banker who was into meditation by the numbers. "Did he tell you how to make the numbers come zinging up out of the lake?" St. James asked.

"Yes," Kenny beamed. "But it's no substitute for

prayer, just plain old prayer. Not whining for help, but thanking God for this moment, this day, and for the promise of eternity."

"I think eternity would be a pain in the ass," said St. James.

Kenny appeared stricken. He set John the Baptist back on the desk. "My gosh, Kiel, you really oughtn't ever talk like that."

Whereas religion was an integral part of Kenny and he exuded it as naturally as breathing, he also exuded bona-fide, day-to-day goodness, the real article. Sometimes it was almost frightening, especially on days like today when the system turned ugly. To find someone who should have been as ornery as any other newsman and to reap the undeniable benefits of his friendship was like discovering a skunk that sprayed Chanel No. 5.

Kenny wanted to know all about new developments in the homicide investigations. So St. James filled him in and said he would bet two-to-one that when the finger-printing was completed it would be disclosed that the culprit was the mayor's son. The editor said that although he was not able to identify his assailant the man was large and extraordinarily strong.

"I hope you're wrong," said Kenny. "My Lord, I taught him in Sunday School when he was only eight. He could recite whole passages of the Bible and loved the stories of Samson and Delilah and David and Goliath. If I re-member his Daddy made him an old-timey slingshot and he brought it to class to show the other youngsters what David used against the Philistine giant."

"You sure about that?" St. James almost gibbered with excitement. "You sure it was him?"

"Almost," Kenny said." I have a pretty good memory and I'm almost certain."

154

"Great jumping balls of shit," said St. James. Wait until the good captain hears of this. Surely he would fingerprint Rudell first and be done with it, writing the final chapter to this interminable, frustrating mess which had boomed sales of burglar-bars and handguns and put the fear of God into the residents of Catherine.

"I wish you wouldn't talk like that," said Kenny, flipping his chocolate-drop eyes from side to side the way he did when he was distressed.

"I'm glad you're back," said St. James. "I got to phone Orson."

"Why do you look like that, Kiel? Is anything wrong? Can I help in any way?"

"You already have, Benny—believe me, you already have."

Boles, of course, was not in his office.

His secretary said that two kids out in Westcrest, the high-mortgage district, had blown themselves to bits playing with a high-explosive shell they'd apparently found on the artillery range of Camp Davenport. The explosion totaled a carport and wrecked the side of a brick house the size of a Holiday Inn.

"Why didn't he call me?" St. James said nastily to the secretary. "Did he call the TV?"

"I don't know, he was in an awful hurry. The demolition technicians from the camp are there with him. There's another shell that didn't explode and they are going to take it to the camp and blow it up."

"Hold on a minute, Reba," St. James said, screaming then at Brenda Keeton who was doing a piece on the Police and Firemen's Benefit Dance. He told Brenda what had happened and instructed her to get out to Westcrest on the double and cover it. She seemed reluctant to leave the unfinished piece in her VDT and St. James snarled, "Forget that crap and get your ass to Westcrest."

When she departed he said to Boles's secretary, "I just wish to God you people would call us on stuff like this."

"It's not my fault," said Reba.

"I don't give a rat's ass who's fault it is, just *call* us."

"You've got no call to talk to me that way," said Reba, hanging up in his face.

By the end of the day he no longer was a hero to practically anybody he knew, which suited him fine. He could cope with anger, even hatred, but did not have the foggiest idea how to respond to admiration.

That evening he finally managed to locate Boles at home and the captain of detectives said there had been no time to get in touch with the newspaper. "This the third time in two years that people have killed theirself from collecting brass at the camp," Boles said. "Be glad you didn't have to see this one—Brenda puked on my sleeve."

"Of course you phoned TV," St. James said. "We'll see you on the six o'clock news in full color looking like Robin Hood."

"I just like green, hoss."

"Did you call TV?"

"Nope."

Mollified, St. James asked about the fingerprinting and told him what Kenny had said about Rudell. Boles said he had already fingerprinted him, also Johnny Trask and Robert Goodbee. None of the prints matched those on the handle of the jackknife.

"What about Dillard Harmon?"

"He's sick in bed. I think he drinks heavy at night and also he's just about got to be pussy-whipped."

"Do you think he's our man?"

"It's possible hoss," said Boles, weariness in his voice. "Anything's possible."

Feeling suddenly contrite, St. James asked, "How's your wife?"

"She's hurting, it's an awful thing to say, but if she's got to die to quit hurting, I want her dead, bless her heart."

"I'm sorry, Orson."

And Boles said, "Me, too. It's a dirty thing, hoss, to watch somebody you love just lying there rotting to pieces."

"Can I do anything?"

"Thank you, hoss, there ain't a thing to do that hadden been did."

When he hung up the phone St. James went into his kitchen and poured three fingers of I.W. Harper in a Kraft cheese glass and drank it neat. He had a pot of fresh chili bubbling on the stove and a fresh box of Sunshine soda crackers on the refrigerator, but he was not hungry. Somebody was playing "Stardust" on the clock-radio in his bedroom and it made him think of May and the way it was when they first fell in love. So very long ago and yet only yesterday. The only time he truly missed his former wife was when he heard music they had shared and then the old feelings welled up in him and he remembered. The first time he ever danced with May he had been working on a drilling rig in the Atchafalaya River and when the pipe stuck in the hole the crews were allowed to go home a few days. May had her shiny brown hair braided in a kind of crown on top and there was sparkly stuff sprinkled on the braid so that it twinkled in the pink light. He was twenty-two and hoping for a newspaper job, any kind of newspaper job that would give him a chance to use his college major in journalism. May was eighteen and hadn't finished school; and the sweetness of "Stardust" was in their heads and May had

157

stardust in her hair. It was a shame people in love no longer had straight-out sweet music to hang their memories from. How could a kid feel that absolute thrill while watching Michael Jackson tippytoe around and screw the air? He considered phoning May, but knew that she would be drunk or at least half drunk.

He sat for a time on the porch thinking of Boles and Boles's wife and of the investigation. From time to time, for no reason he could understand, he conjured a clear vision of the jackknife Orson handed him when he was in the hospital. The knife the man left on the roof after Crystal zapped him. Worn brown-and-cream bone handle and narrow blade. The Case trademark engraved on an oval plate affixed to the handle. Brass showing through silvered fittings at each end of the handle and solid brass liners. A squiggly streak of tar near the point of the blade. He knew that in his lifetime he'd seen at least a dozen such knives. They were not altogether commonplace but you could buy one at most sporting goods stores if you needed a knife with a single blade.

He went inside and found his motorcycle helmet, a new silver-gray one that made his head look like the nose of a bullet. The clear plastic shield was still stained where he'd forgotten and spit tobacco juice. He stopped and wiped it out but it needed more attention and now he took the garden hose to it in front of the house. The motorcycle was parked on the sidewalk leading to the front steps. He was squirting water inside the mask when one of the gay young men next door came outside and saw him, watched awhile, shrugged and returned inside. The gays were nice people and he liked them and enjoyed talking with them when they weren't hammering on the inside of their rented home, but it was clear to him they thought he was a bit odd, riding a hot Honda FT 500 at his age and coming and going with Crystal all hours of the day and night. The young man probably figured St. James squirted water regularly into his helmet. St. James grinned as he cleaned the mask. His neighbors likely would not be surprised if he lay on his back beside the Honda and poured gasoline in his mouth.

He rode the bike downtown in the gathering dusk and turned right out North Main past the Coca-Cola plant and the baby-powder factory and across the Texas & Pacific tracks. When he crept past Dillard Harmon's house the mechanic was standing on the front porch in a pair of pajama pants, a can of beer in his hand. His flat belly was ribbed with muscle and his forearms looked huge. St. James waved at him but Harmon only stared at him and did not return the wave.

Stephanie was not on the porch. Perhaps she was inside doing pushups with her tongue.

St. James phoned Boles's house to tell him that if Harmon was well enough to drink beer and walk around he was well enough to be fingerprinted, but a private nurse answered the phone and said that Mr. Boles was called out on business and she did not know when he would be back.

"How is Mrs. Boles doing?"

"She hurts," said the nurse. "The pain-killing injections don't seem to help. I'll tell Mr. Boles you phoned. Do you want him to return the call?"

"Thank you, no, he's got enough on his mind."

"He's so sweet to her," the nurse said. "I never saw a man that tender."

159

21

"HE WON'T COME OUT A HIS HOUSE," SAID ORSON BOLES. "I know he ain't sick, but we can't *drag* him out."

"You could take the fingerprint kit to his house and do it there," said the district attorney.

Boles sighed and said, "Okay, okay; but his wife told me he didn't want no police on the premises and I don't like to push in there. Dillard and me went to school together—and he keeps all our worn-out cop cars running."

"Boles," said the district attorney, who had pig's ears and no neck, "sometimes I get the feeling you're dragging your feet on this."

"What I'm dragging is my ass," Boles said. "I'm seven months behind on my sleep."

"It's about time you gave something we can take to court. I'm getting considerable heat from high places." He raised his one eyebrow, which ran all the way across both eyes, a giant brown caterpillar. Even his forehead was muscular. He could do tricky things with the caterpillar.

"What high places?" asked Boles.

"The governor—the governor's office. They phoned me twice the past week. I kid you not."

"Why?"

"The governor believes it's a bad thing when open season is declared on public servants. And a worse thing when nothing is done about it." The district attorney, whose name was Ripley and who was known among lawmen simply as Kong, could tell you how many pounds the best of the Russians could clean and jerk and recite the name of the strongest man in the world in each weight division, but the truth was that he was not uncommonly bright. He flunked the bar three times before passing and then only after his father was appointed to the state board for bar admissions. "Is the governor's office high enough for you, Captain Boles?"

"We're doing the best we can."

St. James, who had been visiting Boles when the DA arrived in a red-faced snit with his young assistant, said to Ripley: "I don't believe you appreciate the number of hours the captain's working."

The DA eyed St. James for some time and said, "What I don't appreciate is you butting in where you have no business."

"Kiel's my friend," said Boles. "He's worked with me a long time. More than once he's dug up stuff I missed."

"Bully for him," said the DA, and his bespectacled ass-kissing assistant sniggered dutifully. "Captain you show me something soon, something solid that will stand up before a grand jury, or we'll get someone else in here to ramrod the investigation."

"Who's *we*?"

"The mayor and I—that's who's we."

"You mean the mayor's son, the interim mayor."

"Exactly."

"You've talked about this?"

"At length," said the DA. "At con-*sid*-erable length."

Boles looked at the backs of his hands. His ketchup-and-cream skin was all ketchup now, no cream at all. There was a disassembled M-1 rifle on his desk and finally he picked up the greasy clip of cartridges and smelled it as if it were a rose; and he raised his head and smiled his sunniest smile at Ripley. "I tell you what, Ralph, you get your ass out a here or I'm goin' to wrap this here gun barrel 'round your ears."

Ripley left the room, followed by his flunky, fanning the muscles of his back inside a new Haspel summer jacket.

When he was gone, Boles said in an ordinary tone of voice, "I don't think he likes me, hoss."

They sat there at Boles's desk a while, not talking, each thinking his own thoughts. And St. James, remembering the day Barrington was found at the city dump lying on his back in the rain, thought that it seemed a century ago. The razor-sharp three-piece suit and Barrington's Claude Rains face, and Nelson Barton, the coroner-ranger, digging with the blade at the bloody rock. And Nelson had laid the open knife atop a little can while he tried to wipe his hands. The rain washed pink juice from the wound and the rat popped out of the peach can, a very sane, contemplative rat, unafraid, simply going about his rounds. The rat sniffed at the handle of the jackknife. And in the bright rainlight St. James had noticed, without really noticing at all, that a triangular chip was broken from the bone of the handle. A very small chip that exposed the brass liner beneath.

"Let me see the knife from the roof," he said to Boles.

"For what?"

"Just let me see it."

"It's in a envelope, hoss, in one a them cabinets. What's eating you?"

162

"Humor me, Orson."

"Don't I always?" Boles laid the M-1 clip atop the oiled trigger-assembly and after a few minutes located the envelope with the knife. St. James had trouble straightening the metal prongs which held the heavy envelope closed and jammed one of them painfully beneath a thumbnail. He cursed and ripped the entire top off and dumped out the knife among the gun parts on the desk. There was no missing triangle of bone on the handle and he sat there looking at it, afraid to turn it over to the other side, his hand on it, like a stud-poker player who hasn't looked at his hole card, sweating it with two aces showing and a pair of kings across the table.

"When we through with it you can have it," Boles said. "I never knew you to take on so over anything, let alone a wore out pigsticker."

St. James turned the knife slowly over on the desk, closing his eyes until the other side of the handle was exposed. Still holding his breath he saw that near the worn silvery binding where the plate of bone was fitted to the metal, a very small chip was missing. The brass liner shone in a triangle in the gap.

22

IF YOU DID NOT KNOW THAT MIXON'S FUNERAL HOME WAS the fleeting home of the dead, you would think it was the residence of a rich family that had seen too many bad English movies. If you knew it was what it was it still came as almost a surprise to you, no matter how many times you'd seen it. It was a confusing heap of stucco and gables and phony Tudor architecture with brown-stained strips of wood flattened at senseless angles against the walls beneath the eaves. Mullioned windows of beveled glass panes, heavily leaded. Slate roof. Gobs of climbing ivy feeding. Only the snazzy 1983 Cadillac hearse in the gravelled parking area gave it away. A hearse is a hearse. Sleek and silent cousin of the loudmouthed ambulance. Terminal transportation.

The police car crunched to a stop at the side entrance and before they got out, Boles, his hands on the wheel, said, "Kiel, you watch your step, this could be hairy." A second prowl car pulled slowly in behind them, the gravel popping like hot corn beneath the wheels.

"I'll be careful," St. James said to his friend. "You too."

Boles instructed the two patrolmen in the backup car to stay put until he needed them. But almost at once he changed his mind and said no, for them to come inside and wait just inside the door in the small foyer there. "Walk easy, we already made too much noise."

In the foyer were two comfortable-looking chairs and Boles told the policemen they might as well sit down while they waited. The foyer was carpeted in crimson and it was circular with a domed ceiling plastered in pale blue to match plastered walls. It looked like the inside of one of those deep-sea diving bells, except for a stubby flight of stairs leading to the main floor which contained visitation rooms and a sanctuary for services. Once you were inside the building you knew precisely what it was. It smelled of death and useless tears, of posthumous remorse and of the fragrant mockery of dead or dying flowers. Of finality.

"C'mon hoss," said Boles, and they climbed the stairs to a long corridor with an ankle-deep red carpet.

The receptionist had a vase of real roses on her desk. Her long nose twitched as she wrote something on a pad. Except for the twitching she seemed to have the standard, mechanical serenity essential for survival in the environment. She looked up slowly from her writing and said slowly, "May I be of assistance to you, please?"

"Yes, ma'am," said Boles. "I'm trying to get in touch with Nelson Barton."

"I'm afraid he's downstairs," she said. She leaned forward and stuck her nose among the flowers. "Don't you just love American Beauty roses?"

"Yes, ma'am. Can we go on down there and see him?"

"Oh no," she said calmly. "He's in the preparation room, you can't go down there."

"I've been there before," said Boles.

"I'm awfully sorry," she said, "but he just began preparing a body. You'll have to wait until he comes up from the basement."

"How long will it take?"

Pulling her nose from the roses she looked at her watch. "About an hour. It usually takes at least an hour." Then she asked if either Boles or St. James was a relative of the deceased.

"No'm," said Boles. "We found something that Nelson lost. Leastways we think he lost it."

"Oh, well it's mighty nice of you to go out of your way, but rules are rules," she said into the roses, closing her eyes. "What did Nelson lose?"

Boles ignored the question, turning from the desk located in the alcove and moving along a corridor to a descending stairway. With St. James on his heels he moved down two short flights of concrete and steel to the basement.

Nelson Barton, big and balding and blonde, was bending over the naked body of an old woman and apparently he had just rammed the trochar into her abdominal cavity. Blood flowed from the trochar's puncture down her right thigh onto the porcelain top of the embalming table and along the tilted table to the sink.

Nelson resembled the funny one of the Smothers Brothers. He was taller and broader, but when he looked up from the probing point of the trochar he had that tentative, waiting-to-be-ridiculed look.

"How's the old hammer hangin', bub?" Orson asked him, the tone oddly casual in the embalming room. St. James's eyes were drawn irresistibly to the corpse, the two tubes at the base of the neck, one in the jugular, the other in the carotid artery.

166

"Same ole seventy-six," said Barton, smiling his tentative Smothers Brother smile. "Up to my ass in alligators."

"Me, too," said Boles.

"What you need? You got an inquest or something, Orson?"

"Naw, not this time." Moving deliberately, his eyes on Barton's face, Boles reached into a pocket of his green polyester jacket and pulled out the jackknife the police had found on the roof of the bank building. "This yours?"

"What is it?" said the coroner-ranger.

Boles held the closed knife by a tip of the handle, using only the thumb and index finger and waggling it. "Don't you know, bub?"

"It's a knife?"

"Yep."

"What's it to do with me?" said Barton, cutting his eyes right and left as if he expected the walls to break out laughing.

"Put that thing down and wipe your hands," said Boles. "I like you to take a look at this here."

"What for?" Barton pulled out the trochar, which including the handle was approximately two feet long. It looked like an arrow with four cutting edges instead of two, or perhaps a primitive spearhead; the thing was made of stainless steel and from the butt of the handle ran a hose to a faucet in a sink bolted to the concrete wall.

"Don't you know?" said Boles. "Don't you recognize your own knife, Nelson?"

Boles took a step toward Barton, still holding the jackknife, arm extended.

"Git away from me, Orson."

There were three embalming tables side by side in the room, identical, with approximately five feet between

167

them. They could be raised or lowered or tilted on hydraulically operated pedestals. Barton was working on the middle table and the others were vacant. He was pinned between tables, with the captain of detectives and the editor blocking the opening at the head of the table and the wall-sinks sealing off the other end.

"This your knife, Nelson?" said Boles, crooning the words. "This *is* yours, heh Nelson?"

"Stay away from me." Barton began unscrewing the bloody trochar from the length of hose attached to the sink faucet. When finally the thing was free, the perforated steel glistening in fluorescent light, he laid the hose across the belly of the corpse. "I don't want to hurt you, Orson. Don't make me hurt you."

"How 'bout Kiel?" said Boles. "You want to hurt him?"

"No," answered Barton, who was now brandishing the spearhead, still cutting his eyes right and left and all around the room as if the burbling sink and the corpse and the glass-faced cabinet with its assortment of scalpels were about to begin laughing at him. St. James, standing to the left of Boles, half expected Barton to say his mother never *made* biscuits, like in the Kentucky Fried Chicken commercial on TV.

Barton flipped a lever and the table holding the corpse made a hissing sound and began lowering itself until it was about knee-high. Barton leaped lightly over it to stand on the other side of it, holding his weapon against his broad chest, the cutting tip pointed at the ceiling. He said: "And David said to Saul, let no man's heart fail because of him, thy servant will go and fight with this Philistine."

Boles pulled his snub-nosed .38 special from the holster inside his green jacket and said: "It ain't no use to run, Nelson, and I sure hell don't want to put a hole in you."

"So David prevailed over the Philistine with a sling

and with a stone and smote the Philistine and slew him; but there was no sword in the hand of David."

"Come on, Nelson, cut the shit."

"Therefore David ran and stood upon the Philistine and took his sword and drew it out of the sheath thereof and slew him and cut off his head therewith. And when the Philistines saw their champion was dead they fled."

Boles returned the jackknife to the pocket of his jacket. His trigger-finger rested outside the trigger-guard and he held the pistol against the side of his leg. Stink of wet concrete and formaldehyde and something sweet-rotten, faint but definite in the gloom of the long, rectangular basement room. Very little light came through the slits of windows high on the wall where the sinks were bolted. There was an overhead fluorescent light fixture for each table, but the bars of light burned above only the middle table where the old lady lay. One of her gray eyes was open. Her arms were dangling over the sides of the table and long, withered breasts had fallen sideways, a breast under each arm. The tubes in her neck continued to function off the pump, one tube red-black with blood and the other pumping the clear embalming fluid in to replace the blood. It did not look real, but more like a demonstration on a dummy at a school for undertakers. Only the blood running from the hole where the trochar had been looked genuine. That and the trochar itself. It seemed to St. James that the longer he looked at it, the nastier it looked. He was acutely aware of the fact that if Barton got to him and Boles fired wild with the gun, the coroner-ranger could ram the trochar all the way through him. The hose on the floor made sucking noises in a shallow puddle of water.

"If you just steady yourself down," said Boles, "ain't no need for anybody to git hurt."

No answer.

Barton looked from one man to the other, from side to side, not smiling, but almost smiling. A faraway listening look. The precise Tommy Smothers look when Dicky says no one refers to biscuits as being finger-licking good. Just like mother used to make, says the straight man, and now Tommy is about to say, "But mama didn't make me any biscuits."

"Go get the guys upstairs," Boles said then to St. James. "I'm afraid we going to need 'em. Why don't you lay that thing down, Nelson? They ain't no need at all for all this fuss."

St. James started for the staircase, but as he did so, Barton, now clear of the tables, moved with incredible speed to stand between the editor and the stairs. He now held the trochar in front of him, very low, swinging it from hand to hand in the classic stance of the knife-fighter.

"You want me to shoot you, Nelson?" said Boles. "You want me to shoot you in the head?"

"It don't make me no difference."

"Think of your two kids, Nelson. It'll make the hell of a difference to them."

Barton was moving forward now, still stooped, swinging the stubby spear from hand to hand, his eyes on the gun. Boles and St. James, standing shoulder to shoulder, edged backward and Boles raised the gun, holding it with both hands to steady it.

The hose on the floor was sucking air.

"You want to be alive to eat your lunch?" Boles said, gesturing with the stubby gun at a brown paper bag on the shelf beneath the scalpel-cabinet. "What you going to have for lunch, hoss?"

The trochar was still.

Barton appeared to be weighing what Boles had said—wondering whether or not he would be alive to open the bag and remove the sandwiches. Then he shook his head as if to clear it. "And it came to pass that when the Philistine arose, and came and drew nigh to meet David, that David hasted and ran toward the army to meet the Philistine."

"Watch out, hoss!" Boles yelled. "Get behind me, this motherfucker's crazy as a loon."

Barton accelerated the pace toward them, then, wheeling, he headed for the stairs, pulling something from his hip pocket with one rubber-gloved hand, holding the trochar in the other.

When they caught up with him he was standing in the center of the gravelled parking area, the trochar at his feet. Sunlight winked from the four cutting edges of the murderous tool. Barton fitted a stone into the pocket of a sling. "And the men of Israel and of Judah arose and shouted and *pursued* the Philistines . . . and the wounded of the Philistines fell down by the way to Shaaraim, even unto Gath and unto Ekron." Barton began whipping the rawhide thongs round and round over his head as Rudell Link had done at the lake. St. James, hating himself, turned his back to the singing stone and bent over so it wouldn't catch him in the back of the head.

Boles's .38 special cracked once, the noise startling in the quiet. When St. James turned he saw Barton grimacing with pain, releasing the rock with a final snap of the pocketed whip. You could not see the stone in flight, only hear it, and St. James, dropping to his belly in the gravel and still hearing the silken swish of the stone, still feeling the coolness of its passage on his cheek, yelled, "For Christsake, Orson, stop him."

And Boles said quietly, almost conversationally, "Nelson, don't load that thing. You hear me?"

Barton, reloading, had been hit in the left shoulder,

171

the blood spreading rapidly in the blue cloth of the shirt. His rubber apron covered a portion of the stain. "And when Saul saw David go forth against the Philistine, he said unto Abner, the captain of the Host: 'Abner, whose son is this youth? And Abner said, 'As thy soul liveth O King, I cannot tell.' "

He now had the trochar in the belly-pocket of the waterproof apron, the handle of it in easy reach if they tried to rush him. And again he began the rhythmic business with the stone, each whirl slightly faster than the one before.

"Okay, Nelson," said Boles. "You won't hear my next shot. I'm going to blow your goddamned nose off for ya."

And then Barton began sobbing, dropping the rawhide sling and stone, ripping the stainless steel dagger from the pocket of the apron and hurling it into a ligustrum bush near the side entrance of the building. He buried his face in his hands and fell to his knees in the gravel, the sobs racking him, shoulders jumping.

"Hands behind your head," said Boles, almost gently. And gently he manacled the shaking wrists of the big, blonde man. "Why'd you kill them, hoss?" he murmured. "Why'd you have to go and kill somebody?"

When Barton had been loaded, weeping, into the detective's car, Boles got on the intercom and asked what had become of Beeson and Wicks, the two men he'd left in the foyer. The radio dispatcher said a train had hit a school bus on the edge of town. "Oh my God," said Boles. "I hate this fucking job." He stared at the tracks where the backup car had been parked behind them and said, "I hate it, hoss, I truly hate it."

23

THAT EVENING THE THREE OF THEM, BOLES, CRYSTAL, AND St. James, celebrated with steaks and lobster and quantities of almost-frozen Heineken. During the meal they had little really serious conversation, but now, as they sat stuffed and a little tight, gazing at their gnawed T-bones, the captain of detectives held court. Contrary to his everyday enthusiasms he wore a navy flannel blazer and medium-gray slacks with cordovan tassel-loafers. His heavy-jawed face was a study in controlled excitement. Missing almost entirely, almost but not quite, was his redneck language—which ordinarily he adapted to his audience.

"What we are celebrating here tonight," he beamed, "is the end of a mess which almost cost the newshound his life, me my job, and Miss Crystal a very close friend."

"Very close," Crystal giggled, well on her way to a super-high. These super-highs as a rule were considerably profitable for St. James. Her hand was on him under the table. Her touch was very light, somewhat rotary so that she rolled the erection against his leg. He sought to hold a straight face for Boles, even though he recognized that Boles knew damned well what was happening beneath the table of the darkened booth.

"As I told you earlier," Boles pontificated, turning on the resonance, "Nelson Barton is the grandson of Bob Goodbee. There was nothing on the minutes of the city council meetings about it, but Barton learned that the mayor and Commissioner Barrington were set to evict the old man from the shack at the city dump. There are only three votes on the council and their two votes would've done it.

"The council had been threatening the old man with eviction for years. I have no notion why Goodbee preferred living alone in the shack in all that filth, eating rats. He didn't have to. The daughter in New Orleans wanted him to live with her—and Nelson, her son, had begged Goodbee to come live with him and his wife and children.

"No soap.

"Goodbee was, and is, of a mind that independence is more important than soap and water and three squares a day."

"Why didn't he use the funny little shower he had rigged to the cistern behind the shack?" St. James wanted to know, now placing his hand on Crystal's to avert almost certain ejaculation.

"He was deathly afraid of getting water in that hole in his chest and strangling to death," said Boles. "Nelson says the old man was even afraid to walk in the rain."

Crystal turned loose of St. James and said, "Nobody knows, really knows, his suffering. I tried to talk with him twice. He made those awful gurgling noises. Once I actually saw the hole when he coughed. You wouldn't believe what it looked like."

"Well," said Boles, "Nelson figured the old man'd

174

suffered enough. And now they were going to bulldoze his home and Nelson simply couldn't abide the thought of it. It was the last straw. On top of Nelson's job as county coroner-ranger, embalmer, and part-time ambulance driver, it flipped him over the edge. He told me he'd reached a point where he was talking to the dead on the slab. He would ask them if he was hurting them. Or he would say to them, 'Now this isn't going to hurt as much as you think.' Stuff like that. He knew for sure he was going bonkers when one day he pulled into a Texaco station for gas and saw a cougar on the hood. The cougar was still there while the filling station man lifted the hood and checked the oil. Another time he saw a bearded giant lying belly-up on a park bench, wearing a brass helmet and shield and shin greaves.

"Strangely, the only time Nelson felt anything akin to peace was out at the dump with his grandpa. Goodbee had a skiff, and sometimes at night they would row out on the sewage-treatment lagoon and just sit there in the moonlight. No talking, just sitting there facing each other for an hour or more."

St. James recalled seeing Goodbee, apparently in earnest conversation, at the lake talking with the young water-skier. "I couldn't hear them," said St. James, "but it looked like Goodbee was talking. He wasn't writing on a pad and I could see his mouth moving and he seemed to be holding onto his throat."

Boles said Goodbee had some kind of electronic device with which he could make sounds a bit like real talking, if he pressed it against his "goozle." The old man rarely used the device. "But he's the one that kept phoning you," Boles said to St. James. "He knew you were working on the case with me; and he wanted to scare us off. He was afraid if he phoned me I'd recognize the goozle-talk."

Crystal took a fresh hold on St. James and began moving it around like the gearshift on her Jag. First, second, third and on up through the gears, failing to get it in reverse because of the bind of his pants. "What about the David and Goliath fixation?" she asked, as if nothing at all were happening under the edge of the redwood table.

"They're David and Goliath buffs," said Boles. "So's the interim mayor, Rudell. It ain't any stranger than panting around Elvis's house in Memphis, or goin' into spasms over Sinatra. When I was a kid I saw an old Gary Cooper movie and I wanted to be Sergeant York for two years. Made me some wrap-leggings, tongued my thumb and fanned it over the sights on my Crosman air rifle."

"Goodbee was a little old for that kind of thing," said Crystal.

"It started when Nelson was a little kid. He and the mayor's son and the old man formed a kind of half-ass David and Goliath Club. Old man played the giant. Those were better days for him. The three of them would act out the whole thing. Rudell was Saul, or maybe he was Jonathan, I'm not sure. Anyway they got to where they knew the Book of Samuel top to bottom, or pretty close to it. Goodbee would stomp around in his cardboard shin-guards with a wooden sword and a G.I. helmet, threatening to feed Nelson to the birds and carrying on something awful until Nelson finally whacked him with a wad of wet toilet paper. This went on until Rudell was sent off to a private school in Virginia. He flunked out up there and came home to finish his high-schooling. By then he had put on so many airs he wouldn't even discuss David and Goliath and he would cut Nelson cold in public."

"I think that's so sad," said Crystal, turning loose of the gearshift in the nick of time.

"Don't you think it's sad?" she said to St. James.

"Whugh?" he said.

"Whugh?" said Crystal, smiling, the crushed-glass gaze full upon him in the lavender gloom of The Iron Hog.

"I mean, what? I lost track."

"I can understand how he lured Barrington to the city dump," St. James said. "Barrington was in charge of the dump and of the landfill there, even the lagoon—but how in God's name did he get the mayor up in the city courtroom?" said Crystal.

"He said there was termites and he wanted to show the mayor how some a them ate right through the railing that separated the bench from the spectator seats. The mayor was scared to death of termites. Nelson heard him talking one day to someone at the funeral home, heard him say that termites didn't make any noise at all and you didn't even know they were around till they chewed everything to dust and popped out in plain sight."

"You've got to be kidding, Orson," said St. James, his voice relieved. He had believed that Crystal was intent on jerking him off under the table. He held her now by the wrist as he sought for a normal tone of voice. "And what about the roof? Why the rocks off the roof?"

"Nelson can't explain that, except to say they were pretty; and that a long time ago some of the gravel was loose on the roof and he and Rudell would go up there and fill their pockets with the smooth frosted quartz pebbles. They weren't stuck in the tar then. Nelson's dad was a chiropractor on one of the floors, so they had a kind of excuse. And they would look out across the river at the Firwood Cemetery and eat powdered malt with Johnny Trask."

"Malted milk," said St. James.

"Yes, Johnny's dad was a dentist and he got little sample jars from Horlick's. Back there they thought the stuff

177

was good for the teeth." Boles took a long pull on his icy beer. There was a pitcherful on the table of the booth and he poured beers all around.

And St. James, smiling at his old friend, thought of what Trask said about sticking his tongue into the jar until it was gummy. And the editor thought then that Boles was sure to wink and say, "Bottom's up, kids, we can't fly on one feather."

And Boles winked and said, "Drink her down hoss, man can't sail on one wing."

Crystal laughed as if this were just about the funniest thing in the world, again seizing St. James by the head of the penis and fondling him, shifting him, rotating him with as much lateral motion as the corduroy slacks allowed.

"So where did Nelson get a key to get onto the roof the other night?"

"It was in his dad's possessions. Nelson inherited a ring full a keys and a Desoto sedan when his dad died, about a year after Miz Barton passed on."

"Why'd he have a hard-on for me?" said St. James. "He like to conked me in the parking lot at Mixon's."

"You were with me both times, in the courtroom and at the dump. He associated you with the investigation. And you wrote that editorial calling the killer a 'cowardly, crazy creep.' Nelson may be a creep. But he damn sure ain't no coward." Boles slipped back into the cornpone now, looking very sad. "What he ain't most is a coward."

"Do you think he'll do any hard time?"

"I don't think so. He's definitely sick in the head. And the defense will get ole Bob Goodbee on the stand whistling through that raw hole and trying to talk with that goozle gadget. And they'll show photographs of embalmers at work. Job stress and all that. I figure it's the funny farm, the rubber room, for Nelson. He'll be out walking around in a few years."

"But he killed those men," said Crystal. "And he tried to kill Kiel, too."

"Miss Crystal, that would have been the biggest step for journalism since Gutenberg done his thing with movable type." Boles stared at the bone on his plate and belched. He poured another round from the sweating glass pitcher.

"Thanks," said St. James, clutching at Crystal's round wrist.

"Thing that stumps me most," said the detective, "is your hunch he would show on the roof of the Mobley. Waddaya figure the odds against him coming on that particular night?"

"Who knows?" St. James could still feel the bite of the knife in his ribs. The skin was tight along the line of incision. "I still say it's no weirder than someone holding the winning ticket in a lottery where they sell ten million tickets."

"Maybe not, I got to get home to my old lady and run off that private nurse for the night. She's sweet, but she bosses me. 'Pick that up. Put this over here. Go wash your hands.' You know?"

With Crystal on the back end of the Honda FT 500 Ascot and both of them feeling little pain after sharing three pitchers of beer, they headed for St. James's house on Timothy Lane.

It was about eleven o'clock.

There had been a mild sprinkling of rain and the old brick streets glistened, giving texture to the weak fall of streetlight. St. James kept it in low gear as they putt-putted down Sycamore Drive past the St. Luke's Baptist

179

Church. "Lookit," said Crystal in his ear. "Let's try the side door. It may be unlocked again."

"We went in the front door."

"Front door, side door, what difference?" She wriggled, disturbing the smooth balance of the bike.

He turned around in the street and coasted the bike into the parking lot, leaving it in low gear but squeezing the clutch so that it would roll into one of the yellow-painted slots. They walked around to the front door and it was locked fast. Then they went along the side of the building to a little porch and tried the door there. It swung open silently on oiled hinges.

"You're going to get in the tank again?" asked St. James, hearing his own words boom back at him from plastered walls.

"Yes," said Crystal, "into the tank."

"You know what it means if we're caught. There *has* to be somebody in the building."

"Who cares?"

"Not me," he was amazed to hear himself say, feeling then the full lift of the beer and two pre-dinner bourbons. He felt very light and he seemed to be expanding and filling a hell of a lot of space.

And they were in the baptismal tank in their clothes and a great rumbling voice seemed to say from the ceiling, "Go ahead and do it son. It is so written. So shall it *be*."

"In your *tank*, sir?"

"Yea, verily."

And so he did.